SCAVENGER ATTACK

Marcus dove for the asphalt as the figures closing in from both sides opened up. Bullets buzzed overhead and thudded into the road. Without a break in his motion, he rolled to the left, presenting as difficult a target as possible, swiveling and aiming at the attackers surging from the woods on his side of the highway. He aimed and fired on the move, and he was gratified to see three foes drop—and then he knew what they were.

The dozens of ambushers charging from the forest were scavengers, a large band of predatory wanderers who preyed upon everyone they encountered. Scavengers were the bane of the postwar era, as prolific as the large rats that inhabited the underground sewers and tunnels in the cities. The Outlands were infested with both.

Marcus shot two more, continuing to roll, never lying still for a second. To do so would mean his death.

Shabbily attired, many in filthy rags, and armed with everything from pitchforks to lever-action rifles, the scavengers screamed and bellowed as they rushed the Warriors.

Also in the *Endworld* series by David Robbins:

#21: BOSTON RUN
DAVID ROBBINS

LEISURE BOOKS   NEW YORK CITY

Dedicated to:
Judy, Joshua and Shane.
Mark, Brenda, Danielle and Jeremiah.
Karen, Mike and Keith.
And Don, Chris, Erin and Amber.
Oh.
Let's not forget T.H.E. CAT.

A LEISURE BOOK®

May 1990

Published by

Dorchester Publishing Co., Inc.
276 Fifth Avenue
New York, NY 10001

Chapter One

His grey eyes snapped open with the abruptness typical of those who were brought back from the dead, and he stared at the yellow ceiling overhead in a state of dazed bewilderment. Where am I? was the first question his mind posed. He tried to lift his arms, but for some reason they wouldn't budge. What happened? was his second question. He knew he was lying on his back on a soft surface, although he couldn't remember how he got there. His throat felt extremely dry, so he swallowed and licked his lips.

"Ahhhhhh. I see our patient is finally awake," said a low, kindly voice from somewhere off to his left. "How are you feeling?"

He blinked when a white-haired man materialized above him, noting the man's lined, mature countenance and steady blue eyes. "Wh—" he croaked, trying to speak, his parched throat and strangely immobile jawbone strangling the word and causing him to cough.

"I'm Doctor Milton," the man said, introducing himself.

He realized the man wore a smock and had a stethoscope in

an upper pocket. He attempted to raise his head, but couldn't.

"I'll get you a glass of water," the physician offered, and disappeared.

Footsteps and the sound of running water reached his ears. and he waited expectantly for the doctor to return, striving to concentrate, to attain mental clarity. There were so many questions he needed answered.

"Here's your water," Doctor Milton said, returning with a small glass in his left hand. "Open your mouth and I'll pour."

Gratefully, he complied and felt the cool liquid trickle over his tongue and down his throat.

"You mustn't drink it too fast," the doctor advised, tilting the glass carefully and slowly until the last drop was gone. "There. Now you should feel a little better."

"I do. Thanks," he replied, then addressed the physician in a rush, apprehension seizing him. "Why couldn't I do it myself? What's wrong with me. Why can't I move?"

"There, there. Calm down," Doctor Milton said, and patted him on the right shoulder. "You can't move because your jaw, arms, and legs are under restraint for your own good. You were in a serious accident and you're in the hospital."

"An accident?" he repeated quizzically.

"Yes. Don't you remember?"

"No."

"Well, severe trauma often induces a form of amnesia. It's a technique the brain uses to protect us from memories too terrible to bear," Doctor Milton stated.

"What happened?"

Doctor Milton pursed his lips. "Are you certain you want to know?"

"Yes," he responded, striving to recall the accident but drawing a blank. "Please."

"I don't know," Doctor Milton said hesitantly. "I don't want to trigger a relapse. You only came out of your coma yesterday, and the few times you've been awake you were incoherent."

"I was in a coma!" he exclaimed.

"For three months."

The revelation staggered him. He closed his eyes, his mind awhirl. "I don't remember."

Doctor Milton chuckled. "Of course you don't."

"What happened?" he asked again, opening his eyes. "You must tell me."

"I don't know."

"Please," he urged.

The soft-spoken physician studied the patient for a moment, then twisted and deposited the glass on a stand next to the bed. "All right, although it's against my better judgment." He gazed at the man in the bed. "Three months ago you were working on a demolition crew in Wakefield. You were operating a bulldozer and you were in the process of tearing down an abandoned building when something went wrong. A brick wall collapsed on top of you, and you were pinned under the rubble for over an hour before your coworkers could dig you out. Then you were rushed here for emergency treatment." He paused. "You nearly died. The surgeons operated on you for ten hours, trying to repair your grave head wound. If there had been a few more bricks on top of you, your skull would have been crushed completely."

"I don't remember," he reiterated in a strained tone.

"Count yourself fortunate if you never do," Doctor Milton said. "You've had virtually no detectable brain activity for three months. Technically, from a legal standpoint, you were as good as dead."

"I had no idea," he mumbled, endeavoring to recall the thinnest thread of memory, anything that would confirm Milton's statements. But why, he wondered, should he be suspicious of the physician?

"You'll have a long road to recovery," Doctor Milton remarked. "There will be many hours of therapy involved. Even after you're released from the hospital, you'll be on an outpatient basis for a year, minimum."

"What's the name of the hospital?" he asked absently, struggling to comprehend the implications.

"I'm sorry. I should have told you before. You're in Kennedy Memorial Hospital."

"Kennedy Hospital?"

"Yes. You know. There were several famous Kennedy brothers who lived before the war. One of them became the President of the United States. Another became Attorney General, I believe. And the third one was . . ." Doctor Milton said, and stopped, scratching his chin. "Funny. I can never remember what the third one did to deserve having a hospital named after him. This was known as Massachusetts General Hospital until it was renamed in his honor."

"Was I ever here before?"

"No, I don't believe so. Why?" Doctor Milton inquired.

"Because I don't remember anything about this hospital."

"Give yourself time."

"Where's it located?"

The doctor seemed surprised by the query. "You don't know in which city you are?"

"No. Should I?"

"By all rights, yes," Milton said. He leaned over and examined his patient's gray eyes. "As I mentioned before, amnesia triggered by a startling experience is quite common. Forgetting about your accident, for instance, isn't unusual. Even forgetting a few minor details about your life wouldn't be out of the ordinary. But forgetting the name of the very city in which you were born and raised is highly irregular." He straightened and frowned. "We shall begin a series of tests immediately."

"Can you remove the restraints?"

"Certainly. I'll have a nurse attend to it in a minute," Doctor Milton said. "But first I want to ask you a few questions. Do you feel up to them?"

"I guess so," he replied, still feeling extremely confused.

"Do you know the names of your parents?"

The patient considered the query for a full minute before responding. "No."

"Hmmm. What year is it?"

Again the patient pondered for a while, then shook his head.

"I have no idea."

"How many years has it been since the war?"

"What war?"

"World War Three, of course."

His forehead furrowed and he stared at he ceiling. "I don't know."

Doctor Milton shook his head. "I didn't anticipate this. I'm afraid you'll require more extensive therapy than I indicated. We must gauge the full extent of your amnesia, Mister Berwin."

The patient blicked a few times. "Berwin?"

Shock etched deeper lines in the physician's face. "Don't you remember your own name?"

"I . . ." the patient began, and grimaced as if in pain. "Dear Spirit! No! I don't know my name!" he exclaimed.

"Stay calm," Doctor Milton reiterated. "I'm sure your condition is only temporary."

Berwin shifted his eyes from side to side. "This isn't right."

"What isn't right?"

"I don't know," Berwin said. "I can't put my finger on it."

"After what you've been through, I'm not surprised you're disoriented," Milton remarked. "As the saying goes, though, time heals all wounds. Give yourself time. Lots of time."

Berwin sighed and looked at the doctor. "Will you have the restraints removed now?"

Doctor Milton nodded and departed. Somewhere a door closed.

The man named Berwin knit his brow in perplexity and racked his brain for a memory, *any* memory, of his past. A flurry of jumbled images surfaced and promptly evaporated, as insubstantial as the air he breathed, upsetting him immensely. How could he forget everything about himself? Even his own name! How was it possible for a person to lose his identity, yet remember how to communicate, how to converse and understand others? He didn't know who he was, but he knew the English language. What else did he know? Two plus two equaled four. The moon orbited the earth. The Bowie knife qualified as the most superb blade ever constructed.

Berwin frowned, puzzled by his train of thought. Why in the world would he think of Bowie knives at a time like this? he asked himself. Was he a knife collector? He envisioned a pair of Bowies in his mind's eye and became oddly excited. But before he could reflect on the implications he heard a clicking noise, which he assumed to be a doorknob turning, and a second later a cheery female voice greeted him.

"The doctor just told me the good news, Mister Berwin. I'll have those restraints off in a jiffy."

He smiled at a pretty brunette attired in a white uniform who appeared on his right side. Her brown eyes regarded him in a friendly fashion. "Hello," he said.

"Hello yourself, handsome," she responded, and gave him a playful wink. "I'm Nurse Krittenbauer, but you can call me Nancy."

Berwin judged her to be in her thirties, a competent professional who thoroughly enjoyed her work. "I'm pleased to meet you, Nancy."

"Oh, we met months ago," she replied as she began unfastening the strap securing his jaw. "I've looked in on you several times each shift, six days a week, for the past three months. I've taken your pulse more times than I can remember. I've bathed you and changed your hospital gown." She snickered. "I know everything there is to know about you."

Suddenly his jaw was free, and he opened his mouth as far as he could and raised his head to discover he was in an immaculately clean room with white walls and a tiled floor.

Nancy went to work on the straps binding his arms. She glanced at him and chuckled. "Are you practicing to swallow an apple whole?"

"My jaw feels as if it's made of lead," Berwin replied, and opened and closed his mouth several times, stretching his jaw and neck muscles, relieving the stiffness caused by prolonged immobility.

"I'll bet it does," Nancy said. She loosened the restraint of his right arm, then walked around the bed and began to undo the strap on his left. "I can imagine how antsy you must be to get up and move about, but you're to stay put until Doctor Milton returns. Is that understood?''

Berwin nodded, staring at the loose-fitting green gown in which he was clothed. He saw his naked feet sticking up at the end of the bed. Looped around his ankles were wide black straps.

"After being confined for so long to your bed, you'll need to recuperate slowly," the nurse continued. "Don't push yourself. Take it easy. Give yourself time."

"The doctor said the same thing," Berwin commented.

"That makes it official," Nancy quipped. She freed his left arm and stepped to the foot of the bed.

Berwin propped himself on his elbows and rotated his head from right to left, limbering his neck muscles some more. Suddenly vertigo afflicted him, swamping his consciousness in a flood of dizziness, and he collapsed onto his back.

"Are you okay?" Nancy inquired.

"I'm a little lightheaded," Berwin admitted.

"Just lie there and breathe deeply," she directed him.

He obeyed, and gradually the vertigo subsided, leaving a lingering feeling of weakness in its wake. His stomach unexpectedly growled.

"Is there a lion under the bed or are you hungry?" Nurse Krittenbaur asked.

"I'm starved," Berwin abruptly answered.

"I'll ask the doctor if you can have solid foods. We've been feeding you intravenously since you lapsed into the coma," she said, and finished unfastening the straps. "There."

Berwin wiggled his toes and moved his feet in small circles, restoring his circulation. He lifted his left arm and inspected the crook of his elbow. Several puncture marks were spaced close together over his most prominent vein.

"Did the doctor say anything about notifying your mother and father?" Nancy queried.

"My mom and dad are alive?" Berwin responded in surprise.

"Sure. They've visited you practically every day. Why do you look so stunned?"

"I don't know. Doctor Milton mentioned them, but for some reason I assumed they were dead."

"Did he mention your sister?"

Berwin rose onto his elbows again, his mouth slack, flabbergasted. "I have a sister?"

The nurse smiled. "Yep. She's six years younger than you are, I believe."

"I didn't know," Berwin said sadly.

"Doctor Milton told me about your amnesia. Don't take it too hard. I've seen many patients who couldn't remember people and places, and they all recovered. You'll be fine."

"I hope so," Berwin commented softly, and lay down. He covered his eyes with his left forearm. "I'd like to be alone, if you don't mind."

"No problem," Nancy said. "I'll check with the doctor on your food. You may have to take some tests first. Just don't move."

"I won't."

"Promise?"

"I promise," Berwin assured her.

She walked to the door, glanced at the forlorn patient for a moment, and exited the room, stepping into an immaculate, deserted corridor. Humming to herself, she strolled to the right, and she was less than eight feet from a junction when around the corner came Doctor Milton. They halted a yard from each other.

"Did you remove the restraints?" the physician asked.

"Yes," she responded dutifully.

"You talked to him?"

"Yes."

"And?" Doctor Milton prompted impatiently.

Nurse Krittenbauer smiled maliciously. "You were right. We don't need to worry. The stupid son of a bitch doesn't suspect a thing."

Chapter Two

Ten yards from the cabin he heard the low sobs and sniffling coming through the open window situated to the right of the front door and paused. The pitiable crying filled him with sorrow, and he had to force himself to walk up to the door and knock. He pasted a grin on his face and hooked his thumbs in his gunbelt.

No one answered the knock.

He debated whether to try again or leave. She might want to be alone, and the last thing he wanted to do was contribute to her sadness. But he had volunteered to bring her the news. As much as he disliked the notion, he had to tell her.

The sobbing came through the window, unabated.

He knocked louder the second time, using his knuckles to pound on the door. Predictably, the crying ceased.

"Who is it?" she called out.

"It's me, Jenny. Hickok," he informed her, and nervously ran his right hand through his long blond hair, then stroked his sweeping mustache.

"Just a moment," she said.

Hickok could imagine her dabbing at her eyes and checking her appearance in a mirror. He glanced idly down at his buckskins and moccasins, wondering if it was too late for him to head for the hills.

The front door opened.

"Hello," Jenny said, greeting him, bravely mustering a wan grin. Her green eyes bored into his blue ones. Luxuriant blonde hair fell past her slim shoulders. She wore a pale green blouse and faded, patched jeans. "Have you heard any news?"

"That's why I'm here," Hickok answered, and rested his hands on the pearl-handled Colt Python revolvers riding in a holster on each hip.

Anxiety contorted Jenny's face and she placed her hands on his upper arms. "Well?"

"I don't know how to tell you this," the gunman said with a heavy heart.

"Out with it," Jenny urged, shaking him. "Please."

"All right," Hickok said, and took a deep breath. "They took him away in a helicopter."

The words seemed to shrink her before his eyes. She released him, her arms dropping to her sides, her chin drooping to her chest, her posture bowed as if under an enormous weight. "There's no chance of a mistake?" she asked almost in a whisper.

Hickok wished that he'd let someone else offer to tell her. "No chance," he assured her.

"I was afraid of this," Jenny said.

"It doesn't mean he's dead," Hickok declared, and immediately regretted his rashness when she looked up at him, a haunted aspect to her eyes. He tried to adopt a lighthearted attitude to lessen her remorse. "I reckon I know the Big Dummy as well any anybody, and I know he'll make it back to us safe and sound."

"Tell me what you found," Jenny stated.

"I didn't find the landing spot myself. The blamed mutants found a field about a mile south of the Home where a helicopter likely landed. At least, from the way all the weeds were bent and broken, and from the impressions left in the soil by the landing gear, we reckon a helicopter was used. We would've found the spot sooner, but the varmints who snatched your hubby were pros. They covered their tracks real well. And they sprinkled buck musk along their trail so the mutants couldn't track them by scent," Hickok detailed, and frowned. "Heck. It took us four days just to find where the coyotes jumped him."

"I know," Jenny said sorrowfully. "I can't believe he's been gone a week already."

"How's your young'un takin' it?" Hickok inquired.

"Gabe cried the whole first day, but he's holding up remarkably well for a boy who isn't quite five years old," Jenny replied.

"I saw him playin' with my sprout a while ago. They were havin' fun," Hickok mentioned, hoping to cheer her by discussing their children. The tactic didn't work.

"Who do you think took him?" Jenny queried, returning to their original subject.

"There's no way of tellin'," Hickok said. "You know how many enemies we've made ever since we made contact with the outside world. Blade has made more than his share. The Technics, the Superiors, the Guild, the Dragons, the Lords of Kismet, or any one of the other cow chips we've stomped are possible suspects. Lynx, Ferret, and Gremlin are still out scourin' the field. Maybe they'll find a clue."

"What if they don't?"

"Don't talk like that. The Warriors won't rest until we discover who took Blade and where they're holdin' him."

Jenny leaned against the jamb and gazed at the trees to the east of the cabin. "I know all of you will try your utmost, and I appreciate your efforts. But I'm also sensible enough to realize that I may never see my husband again. Like you said, he's made a lot of enemies. In his capacity as the head of the Warriors, and in his job as the leader of the Force, he's defeated dozens of power-mongers and crazed killers, some of whom are still alive."

"They'll all get theirs one of these days."

"I miss him," Jenny declared passionately.

"So do I."

She closed her eyes and bit her lower lip.

Hickok stared at her in dismay, at a loss to know what to do, deeply affected by her grief. "How about if I send my missus over to sit with you a spell?" he suggested.

"No thanks," Jenny responded. "I'd rather be alone."

"You shouldn't be by your lonesome at a time like this," the gunman observed. "A person needs friends the most when that person is down in the dumps."

"Meaning me," Jenny said.

"If the boot fits," Hickok joked, then became serious. "We weren't put on this loco world to be alone; otherwise there wouldn't be so many folks traipsin' over the landscape. You have a lot of friends, Jenny, and we're here if you need us."

A glimmer of happiness touched her features. "Thanks."

"So why don't I have Sherry mosey on over for some chitchat?"

"Are you sure she won't mind?"

"Are you kiddin'? Sherry will jump at the chance to get out of our cabin."

Jenny nodded slowly. "Okay. Send her over. I would like someone to talk to."

"On my way," Hickok declared, and pivoted to the right. He beamed and waved and ambled around the cabin, bearing to the south. The instant he was out of her sight his expression clouded. He felt like such a hypocrite trying to convince her to look at the bright side of the situation when, in his own heart, he felt they didn't stand a prayer of locating Blade and bringing him back safely. For one thing, too much time had elapsed since the abduction. For another, whoever took Blade had planned the affair meticulously, which meant they had obviously wanted to specifically grab the head Warrior and no one else. Dozens of Family members used the same route Blade had taken on a daily basis, but the only one kidnapped was him. Why? And who could be behind it?

The gunfighter reflected on the events of the past week as he walked in the direction of his cabin, trying to fit together the pieces of the puzzle for the umpteenth time. Jenny had been right, he decided. It *was* hard to believe seven days had gone by since his pard disappeared.

The first inkling he'd had that something was wrong came when his stocky Indian friend and fellow Warrior, Geronimo, raced up to his cabin and yelled that Blade hadn't returned from Halma and was three hours overdue. As Blade's personal pick to be second-in-command of the Warriors during his absences. Hickok had chosen three other Warriors to accompany Geronimo and himself to the small town located approximately eight miles southwest of the Home. Halma had been abandoned during the war. Six years ago the Family had assisted a large group of refugees from the Twin Cities to settle in Halma, and now the two factions were on the best of terms. The leader of the people in Halma, who called themselves the Clan, was a man named Zahner. Blade and Zahner were close friends. On the day Blade vanished, he'd gone to Halma to visit Zahner.

And never returned.

Hickok selected Beta Triad to help with the search initially. The eighteen Warriors were divided into six Triads of three Warriors apiece. Alpha, Beta, Bravo, Gamma, Omega, and Zulu Triads were, collectively, the fighting arm of the Family, devoted to safeguarding the Home at all costs. Beta Triad consisted of Rikki-Tikki-Tavi, Yama, and Teucer.

The five of them followed the dirt road connecting the Home to Highway 59, then took 59 south to Halma. A quick check with Zahner revealed Blade had departed almost four hours before the other Warriors got there.

The search was on.

After Hickok, Geronimo, and Beta Triad failed to find any trace of Blade, most of the other Warriors and volunteers from the Home and the Clan combed the countryside until midnight, using lanterns, torches, and the few flashlights in their possession.

It was as if the earth had swallowed the head Warrior up.

The next morning they were right back at the job, using every available person, and although they used a thorough grid pattern to cover the terrain, again nothing was found.

Not until the fourth day had Geronimo located the spot where Blade had been captured. Then the mutant Warriors, the three genetically engineered hybrids who comprised Bravo Triad, had tried to trace the trail by scent and been thwarted by the deer musk. Only this very morning had the mutations finally located the helicopter landing site.

Poor Jenny and little Gabe.

Hickok glanced up at the afternoon sun, feeling the warmth on his skin. Ordinarily June was one of his favorite months, with the chill of winter long since gone and the lush spring about to give way to the scorching heat of summer. But he scarcely noticed the scenic splendor of the Home as he hastened to his cabin, engrossed in pondering his friend's abduction.

As near as Geronimo and the hybrids could deduce—and they were the best trackers in the Family—Blade had been walking on the dirt road about three miles from the compound when, for some unknown reason, he'd ventured into the forest to the south of the road. Forty yards into the vegetation was a clearing, and it was there that whoever waited in ambush had jumped the top Warrior. Although the kidnappers had gone to great lengths to eradicate their prints and the signs of a terrific struggle, enough telltale evidence remained to enable Geronimo and the trio of mutations to formulate a plausible scenario.

Hickok simmered at the recollection. Somehow, some way, someone had suckered his pard into the woods and sprung a trap. At least a dozen enemies had been involved, and Blade had put up quite a fight before they'd taken him prisoner. Thankfully, the vermin had wanted Blade alive.

But why? Why? Why?

And who the heck were they?

The notion of Blade being tortured in a dismal dungeon made Hickok's blood boil. If the Warriors could just find one measly clue establishing the identity of the vermin, he'd lead the rescue mission himself. Maybe it was time to call in help, he speculated. Maybe it was time to notify the rest of the Federation.

One hundred and six years after World War Three, the country once known as the United States of America no longer existed. Barbarism reigned where previously a seemingly cultured civilization had prevailed. Disparate organized factions ruled limited areas or certain cities, but the majority of the U.S. was now designated as the Outlands, referring to any and all territory outside of any recognized jurisdiction. In the Outlands life was cheap, survival of the fittest the law of the land. In the Outlands a life span of 30 qualified as exceptional.

But not all of the country had degenerated into darkness and savagery. There were seven organized factions dedicated to preserving the worthwhile vestiges of prewar society, seven factions who had joined in a mutual defense treaty and dubbed themselves the Freedom Federation. Although considerable distances separated many of them, each faction was pledged to dispatch aid to any other member of the alliance when called upon.

Hickok skirted a stand of trees, mulling over which faction he should contact first.

The least reliable in a pinch were the Moles, the inhabitants of a subterranean complex located 50 miles east of the Home. Less than a week prior to World War Three, a group of people who were certain that conflict was inevitable had fled far into the Red Lake Wildlife Management area, where they'd believed they would be safe, and dug a series of underground tunnels in which to live. Those tunnels had later been expanded into the complex, and the occupants had become known as the Moles.

The Clan and the Moles were the only other Federation members who, like the Family, were based in northern Minnesota.

Far off in Montana the Flathead Indians had reclaimed the former state as their own. Finally free of the white man's yoke, they clung to their newfound freedom tenaciously. They had perfected the art of living naturally off the land, and many of them were excellent hunters, trackers, and trappers.

Between Minnesota and Montana, in the area now referred

to as the Dakota Territory, reigned the Cavalry, an army of superb horsemen who were as indomitable as the wild horses they caught and rode.

Embracing a number of Plains and Rocky Mountain states and a few in the Southwest, the Civilized Zone owed its existence to the United States Government, which had relocated to Denver, Colorado, after the Russian attack on the nation's capital. The culture and the standard of living in the Civilized Zone came the closest of any Federation member to approximating the prewar lifestyle—although a pale imitation at best— with one possible exception.

The Free State of California. As one of the few states to retain its administrative integrity after the war, and thanks to its abundant resources, California rated as the most technologically progressive in the entire Federation.

So there they were, Hickok thought to himself, ending his mental review of the Family's allies. Which one should he notify first? Did it even make a difference? Because without a clue as to the head Warrior's whereabouts, the combined might of the Freedom Federation was powerless to free him.

Blade was on his own.

Chapter Three

Berwin had the strangest dream.

He was walking across an expanse of grass toward a peculiar concrete bunker when a blond man in buckskins approached and addressed him.

"Howdy, pard."

"Who are you?" Berwin asked.

The man in the buckskins laughed and slapped his right thigh. "That's a dandy, pard! I reckon that mangy Injun put you up to it, right?"

"Why do you talk like that?" Berwin inquired.

"I don't rightly know what you're gettin' at."

"Why do you use those odd words?"

"Ain't you ever heard Wild West lingo before?"

"No."

"Then your ears are in for a treat. Actually, I like to palaver this way because I'm partial to the Old West. Oh, I went through the same schooling as everybody else, and I can shoot the breeze normal-like if I'm in a mind to, but it tickles my fancy to talk this way and drive that mangy Injun loco!"

The dream abruptly ended and Berwin became aware that someone was shaking his right arm. He opened his eyes and smiled when he saw Nurse Krittenbauer. "Hi, again."

"Hi, handsome. I have your food," she announced, and motioned at a gray cart beside her on which there was a steaming bowl of soup, two slices of buttered bread, and a glass of milk.

"What, no steak?"

"Sorry. But the doctor says you'll have to eat soup for a couple of days, until your stomach adjusts to solids again. In three or four days you might be able to have a steak," Nancy explained.

Berwin sat up. "Bring on the soup. I'm so hungry, I don't care what I get to eat."

"Chicken noodle soup is the soup of the day," Nancy informed him. "Tomorrow you'll get pea soup."

"Yummy," Berwin said dryly.

Nurse Krittenbauer reached down and removed a tray from the second shelf on the cart, then neatly arranged the tray on his lap. "You dozed off again," she commented while she transferred the bowl to the tray.

"I'm bored just lying here. I need exercise."

"Have any interesting dreams?" she inquired offhandedly.

"Nothing much," Berwin responded, leaning forward to sniff the tantalizing aroma from the soup.

"Like what?" Nancy asked as she placed the bread and the milk alongside the bowl.

"I had this strange dream about a really weird guy who talked like he was a reject from the days of the Old West," Berwin divulged, his forehead creasing. "There I go again."

"Beg pardon?"

Berwin looked at her. "Why is it I can remember nonsense about the ancient American West, but I can't recall my own past?"

Nurse Krittenbauer shrugged. "Amnesia works that way, sometimes. Just certain parts of the brain are affected."

"It drives me nuts," Berwin said. He took the spoon she handed him and began eating, savoring every delicious mouthful, pausing long enough to comment, "This is the best chicken noodle soup I've ever tasted."

She smiled. "I bet your mother makes chicken soup just as good."   •

"I wouldn't know," Berwin said, eating contentedly.

Nurse Krittenbauer studied his features for a reaction to her remark. "Because you don't remember a thing about your folks?"

"It's not likely anyone could make soup as tasty as this is," Berwin said.

"Enjoy. I'll be back for the cart in five minutes," she told him, and departed.

Berwin polished off the soup, the bread, and the milk in no time flat. He placed the metal tray on the cart and stretched. The meal had barely served to whet his appetite, and he wished he could have the steak then instead of waiting a couple of days. Still feeling hungry and unaccountably restless, he swung his feet to the cool floor and glanced at the door, which was closed. The nurse would undoubtedly be upset if she found him walking about the room, but he needed to get up and move. The earlier dizziness had cleared entirely, and he was confident he could walk around without aggavating his condition.

"Here goes nothing," he said aloud.

Berwin rose slowly. He tentatively took a step forward, past the cart, delighted at how strong and fit he felt. How soon would they allow him to go outside? he wondered, and turned to gaze out the window situated behind the head of the bed. Something else drew his attention from the window to the left-hand corner.

A closet.

He hadn't noticed the closet before, and curiosity compelled him to step around the bed and investigate. If his clothes and personal affects were in there, they might jar his memory. Any remembrance would be preferable to the clean slate that mocked him every time he probed his mind. He opened the closet door and blinked in surprise at finding it empty.

Where were his clothes?

His glance strayed to the full-length mirror attached to the inner door panel, and he saw himself for the first time since awakening from the coma. Amazement replaced his surprise. He hadn't realized how *huge* he was, easily seven feet in height and endowed with a prodigious physique bulging with layers of rippling muscles. His eyes were gray, his hair dark. The loosefitting gown added to the impression of size, and the sight caused him to compare his appearance to a tent he'd seen once at . . .

Where?

Berwin clenched his brawny hands in anger. For a second, a gut-wrenching second, a genuine memory almost surfaced. He waited, breathing shallowly, hoping to remember, but drew a blank.

"What the hell are you doing out of bed?"

The harsh voice startled him, and he turned sheepishly, as if he was a young boy caught with his hand in the cookie jar. "I wanted a little exercise."

Nurse Krittenbauer stood in the doorway, her displeasure transparent, and pointed at the bed. "Get back in there right now."

Berwin complied, propping his pillow so he could sit upright comfortably, conscious of her watching him.

"What were you doing in the closet?" she asked as she came over to the cart.

"I was hoping to find my clothes. Where are they?"

"Do you have any idea what shape your clothes were in when they brought you here?" Krittenbauer queried, and gave the answer before he could reply. "They were torn up and covered with blood and dirt. Your shirt was ruined, your pants were split down the left leg, and your boots were in pitiful condition. None of your clothing was worth saving."

"Oh," Berwin said lamely.

"I'm afraid I'll have to tell the doctor that you disobeyed orders," she admonished him.

Berwin folded his arms and watched the nurse wheel the cart from the room. If they expected him to remain in bed for more than a few days, they were mistaken. He felt too good, too *healthy,* to stay idle very long. He wanted to get into the swing of things, to return to his job, as soon as he could. The head injury had been sustained three months ago. Surely in . . .''

Head injury?''

Berwin looked at the closet. He couldn't see himself in the mirror from where he sat, but he could recall his image, particularly his hair, and there hadn't been any hair missing or a scar, no evidence whatsoever of the operation he'd supposedly had. He reached up and gingerly ran his right hand through his hair, his fingers covering every square inch. Not until he touched his crown did he discover the scar. His hair had been shaved in a pencil thin horseshoe shape from near the nape of his neck to the top of the head, with the curved contours of the horseshoe conforming to the shape of his crown. He could feel the slight indentation where his skin had been sewn back together. The stitches must have been removed months ago.

So there had been an operation after all.

Puzzled, Berwin folded his hands in his lap. Why was he so suspicious of Doctor Milton? Why did he automatically assume the story about his operation was a lie? Why did he persist in requiring confirmation of every little detail? Was he paranoid by nature? Or was there a deeper, unknown reason? To continue to doubt the physician and the nurse, without a justifiable motivation, would be foolish. And yet he couldn't shake a persistent feeling that something was wrong.

Maybe the problem was all in his head.

Maybe the accident had affected his ability to reason normally.

Berwin sighed and closed his eyes. He'd never been so confused in all his life. But then, how would he know that if he couldn't remember his life? It was no wonder he felt continually frustrated, and his impatience with his condition was growing by the hour. He heard the doorknob turning and opened his eyes.

"What's this about you being out of bed?" Doctor Milton asked as he entered, a clipboard in his left hand.

"I stretched my legs," Berwin responded. "What's the big deal?"

Milton stepped to the side of the bed and wagged the clipboard at his patient. "The big deal is that you could cause a relapse if you overdo it. *I'll* be the judge of what you can and can't do until I'm satisfied you're fully recovered."

"I feel fine," Berwin said defensively.

"Is all the weakness gone?"

"Yes."

"Completely?"

"Yes."

Doctor Milton's eyes narrowed. "Perhaps you are recuperating faster than anticipated, but that doesn't give you the right to defy my instructions. Why are you giving me such a hard time, anyway? Do you think you know more about medicine than I do?"

The question embarrassed Berwin and he fidgeted. "No. Of course not."

"Would you prefer another physician?" Milton asked bluntly.

"No. You're doing a fine job."

"Then let me do my job, please, without having to post a baby-sitter in your room."

"I'll try to not give you any more trouble."

Doctor Milton smiled. "Thank you. I think."

Hoping to change the subject, Berwin nodded at the clipboard. "Did you get the test results?"

"Yes," the doctor replied, and looked at the yellow sheet secured by the metal clip. "I have good news and some not so good news. Which do you want first?"

"Good news would be a nice change of pace."

"Okay. The good news is that there doesn't appear to be any organic damage. Your inability to remember doesn't stem from any contusions in your brain or scarred tissue."

"And the not-so-good news?"

"Is a confirmation of what I originally surmised. The shock of your accident induced your amnesia. Fortunately, the condition is reversible. You could recall every aspect of your life in five minutes, two days, or next month."

"Or next year?" Berwin said.

Doctor Milton nodded. "Or next year. Although personally I believe you'll recover your memory much sooner than that. But rest assured that we will do everything in our power to help you overcome the amnesia."

"What can be done?"

"Associaton with your family and friends will be of immense help," Doctor Milton said. "Amnesia can also be treated by hypnosis and with drugs."

"Drugs?"

"Yes. Sodium amytal and sodium penthothal are sometimes effective in correcting the condition, but I should advise you that the drugs can cause unpleasant side effects," Doctor Milton stated.

"Do you recommend using hypnosis or drugs?" Berwin asked.

"Only as a last resort. I would rather try to jar your memory naturally. We must proceed cautiously. When would you like to begin?"

"How about right now?" Berwin requested.

"Very well. What would you like to know?" the physician asked.

"Everything. Those technicians who administered the tests wouldn't answer any of my questions. They told me to ask you. And Nurse Krittenbauer has revealed very little."

Doctor Milton nodded. "They are performing their jobs properly. I prefer to impart information in a controlled environment, face to face, so I can gauge your reaction. Ask me any question and I'll answer it."

"Where in the world am I?"

"Boston."

Berwin did a double take. "Massachusetts?"

"Is there a Boston somewhere else? You appear to be stunned," Milton remarked.

"I am," Berwin admitted.

"Do you remember anything about Boston?"

"No."

"Give it time," Doctor Milton said. "You were born and

raised right here in Boston, Massachusetts, in the good old United States of America—''

"The United States?'' Berwin said, interrupting in surprise. "What about it?"

"Didn't you say something about a war? World War Three?"

"The United States won the war. You're an American citizen. Quite patriotic too, I understand."

"I am?" Berwin said skeptically. He pressed his hands to his temples as a headache began to bother him.

"What's wrong?"

"I'm not sure. I seem to recall something about the war, but it's vague. I can't put my finger on it."

"Are you experiencing any discomfort?"

"I'm beginning to get a headache," Berwin disclosed.

"Then we'll stop for a while."

"But I want to learn all about my family. I want to see my parents and my sister."

"And I'll arrange for them to visit you in several hours. For now, why don't you lay down and rest," Doctor Milton recommended.

"I'm not tired," Berwin said.

"Rest anyway," Doctor Milton directed. He regarded the giant patient critically as the man reclined. "And under no circumstances are you to get out of bed."

"What if I want to tinkle?"

"Use the urinal bottle under the bed. If you have to go number two, use the bedpan."

"I'm capable of using a bathroom," Berwin stated.

"What do you have against bedpans?" Doctor Milton joked, and chuckled. "Very well. I'll instruct Nurse Krittenbauer to escort you to the bathroom if you have to go."

"Thanks, Doc."

Milton nodded and left the room, insured the door was shut tight, and walked to the right, to the junction where Krittenbauer awaited him. "I was wrong," he informed her. "We do need to worry. His aggressive personality is beginning to assert itself. The damn drug isn't as effective as we'd hoped."

"Or perhaps his will is simply too strong," Krittenbauer speculated. "What do we do now?"

"We expedite the process," Milton said. "You know what will happen to us if we fail."

"Yes," she responded grimly, "and I've never been very fond of firing squads."

Chapter Four

"This is a friggin' waste of time!"

"We're not giving up until we've gone over every foot of ground between the field where the helicopter landed and the road."

"Blade is our friend, yes? We owe him a lot, no?"

The first speaker placed his hands on his hips and glared at his two companions. "Yeah, Blade is our friend and he's done a lot for us," he snapped in a high-pitched, lisping voice. "But that doesn't change the fact we're still wastin' our time. We'll never find a clue." His slanted green eyes were alight with anger. He stood under four feet in height and weighed only 60 pounds, and his entire body was covered with short, grayish-brown fur. His facial features were more like those of a feline than a human; a small mouth sporting wicked teeth, a short nose, a curved forehead, and pointed ears gave him the aspect of a two-legged cat. His only clothing was a gray loincloth.

"We might find a clue if there was less talking and more looking," commented the second member of the threesome. Brown hair three inches long coated his lean frame, which was an inch taller than the cat-man's. A black loincloth covered his privates. An extended nose, tiny brown eyes, and curved ears gave him a weasel-like appearance. "So get looking, Lynx," he added.

"Who died and appointed you our leader, Ferret?" the cat-man retorted.

"Ferret is right, yes?" chimed in the third person. The tallest of the trio, he was five feet ten. His skin was a leathery gray in hue, and he wore a brown loincloth. Unlike his associates, he was hairless. His ears, small circles of flesh, served as counterpoints to his bald pate. A slit of a mouth, bizarre eyes with bright red pupils, and a pointed nose gave him a hawklike visage.

"Who asked you, Gremlin?" Lynx demanded testily.

"No one, no," Gremlin conceded.

"Get off Gremlin's case," Ferret stated. "You're wrong, as uusual, and you're too stubborn to admit it."

"*I'm* stubborn!" Lynx declared.

Ferret made a show of gazing all around them at the surrounding forest. "There must be an echo around here."

"You're the stubborn ones," Lynx said. "You two bozos make me look wishy-washy."

"What's the real reason you're upset?" Ferret asked.

"Figures. All I do is make a point and you're ready to psychoanalyze me," Lynx muttered.

"You didn't answer my question," Ferret noted.

"You know what you can do with your question," Lynx said, and began walking northward along the faint trail they'd been following.

"But Ferret is right again, yes?" Gremlin interjected, walking on the cat-man's heels.

"Is he payin' you to agree with every word he says?" Lynx cracked, glancing over his left shoulder.

"Of course not, no," Gremlin replied.

"What's your beef this time?" Ferret asked, bringing up the rear, his eyes sweeping the ground for anything unusual.

"What do you mean by 'this time'?" Lynx responded. "Are

you implying I gripe a lot?''

"I'm not *implying* you gripe a lot. I'm flat out *telling* you that you gripe a lot," Ferret clarified for him. "In fact, I don't know anyone who does as much complaining as you do. You're never satisfied.''

"Listen to Mister Perfect," Lynx countered. He spied a partial print in the soft soil and halted.

"Did you find a track, yes?" Gremlin asked.

"Yeah," Lynx said, and knelt to examine the imprint. A sigh of frustration escaped his lips. "It's a damn bear track." He stood and continued their trek to the north.

"I wish you would tell us what's eating you," Ferret persisted.

"Why don't you drop the subject?" Lynx suggested.

"Because if we don't get you to spill the beans now, we'll have to put up with your crabby puss until you do.''

"I ain't about to waste my breath tryin' to explain to you two morons," Lynx snapped.

"You shouldn't call us names, no," Gremlin said, his tone conveying his hurt feelings at being insulted.

"Now don't go gettin' misty-eyed on me," Lynx stated. "The three of us are best buddies. I call you a moron because I like you.''

"I'd hate to think of what he'd call us if he *didn't* like us," Ferret quipped.

"You know what I mean," Lynx said.

"No, as usual, we don't," Ferret disputed. "You're talking in circles again.''

"Do you want me to give it to you straight?"

"I don't know if we could take the shock," Ferret replied. Gremlin snickered.

"Okay, you turkeys. I'll lay it on the line," Lynx said, stopping and facing them. "The three of us have been through thick and thin together, right? We were all created in a laboratory by a wacko scientist. Each of us is the product of the ultimate in genetic engineering.''

"Uh-oh. I feel one of his spiels coming on," Ferret observed.

"Déjà vu, yes?" Gremlin agreed.

"Make fun all you want, but you're hearin' me out," Lynx told them. "We all got our start in a rotten test tube. We're all the result of takin' ordinary human embryos and splicing them somehow with animal genes. Each of us is a hybrid."

Ferret yawned loudly. "Yep. Definitely a spiel."

"All three of us rebelled against the Doktor and joined the Family," Lynx said, ignoring the barb. "All three of us have been livin' at the Home for years."

"We should be searching for clues, no?" Gremlin asked.

"We were bored, remember?" Lynx said. "The Family is the nicest bunch of sicky-sweet do-gooders you'd ever want to meet, but we were going stir-crazy."

"Correction. *You* were going stir-crazy," Ferret said, then thought better of his comment. "Correction again. You're crazy anyway, so who could tell the difference?"

"I mean, we were bred to be fighters. We were genetically engineered to be assassins for the lousy Doktor. So it was only natural that we got tired of playin' with the kiddies and huntin' game for the Family to eat. It was only natural we decided to become Warriors so we could add a little excitement to our lives," Lynx stated.

"There you go again," Ferret said. "Where do you dig up these fairy tales? *We* didn't want to become Warriors. You were the one with the brainstorm. You were the one who wanted to be a Warrior, and you were the one who nagged us for months until we finally agreed to go along with your insane scheme."

Lynx frowned. "Some brainstorm I had. We've been Warriors for how long now?"

"Oh, about two years," Ferret answered.

"Exactly. And how much action have we seen in the past two years?"

Ferret and Gremlin exchanged glances.

"Double uh-oh. I suddenly have this sinking feeling that Lynx is about to propose another of his bright ideas," Ferret said.

"Should we run now or later, yes?" Gremlin asked.

"Go ahead. Make fun of me all you want. Get it out of your

systems,'' Lynx commented. ''I want your undivided attention when I reveal my next stroke of genuis.''

''Did he say genius, no?'' Gremlin responded, addressing Ferret.

''I can never get over the fact that his ego and the solar system are both the same size, yes?'' Ferret replied, and immediately regretted imitating Gremlin's unique pattern of speech. When Gremlin had been quite young, the genetic engineer who'd created them, the vile Doktor, had performed an exploratory operation on Gremlin's brain. The Doktor had continually striven to improve his medical knowledge and expertise, and as part of one of his experiments he'd removed a portion of Gremlin's brain and preserved the piece in a jar. As a result, Gremlin always spoke in a bizarre manner.

''My ego has nothing to do with this,'' Lynx declared. ''Fairness is the issue here.''

''Fairness?'' Ferret repeated skeptically.

''Yeah. What have we been doing for the past two years?'' Lynx asked, and expounded in the next breath. ''I'll tell you. We've spent most of our time on guard duty, walkin' the ramparts of the walls enclosing the Home. Every now and then we get to waste a wild animal, like that wolverine we ripped to shreds last month, or we get to tangle with one of those feral mutations, like the black bear with six legs that tried to eat a Tiller. But for the most part we twiddle our thumbs while the other Warriors get to hog all the action.'' He paused and looked at his companions. ''Why should they have all the fun?''

''What are you babbling about?'' Ferret responded. ''The other Warriors spend as much time on wall duty as we do. Every Triad pulls equal eight-hour shifts, and we all get the same number of days off. So how do they hog all the action?''

Lynx beamed, about to disclose the cornerstone of his argument. ''It's simple, Vaccum Head. They get to go on all the runs.''

Ferret and Gremlin looked at one another again.

''This isn't leading up to what I think it's leading up to, is it?'' Ferret asked.

"I think so, yes," Gremlin confirmed.

"I was afraid of that," Ferret said.

"I'm right and both of you know it," Lynx declared. "Who got to go to California? Blade and Hickok. Who went to Seattle? Blade, Hickok, Rikki-Tikki-Tavi, and Yama. Who took the run to Nevada? Blade, Hickok, Geronimo, and Helen. Who went to Florida? Blade, Hickok, and Rikki. Sundance and Bertha have been to Philadelphia. I could go on and on, but you got my point. The other Warriors are allowed to go on extended missions away from the Home, but not us. The other Warriors get to take all the runs, to have all the fun."

"Fun!" Ferret said, and snorted. "Where's the fun in accepting an assignment that could well get you killed? Where's the fun in traveling hundreds of miles from those you love, never knowing if you'll see them again? Where's the fun in finding yourself in a life-threatening situation time and again? Where's the fun in going up against mutations, raiders, scavengers, cannibals, and run-of-the-mill psychopaths?"

"It beats wall duty," Lynx remarked.

"You want *us* to go on one of the runs, yes?" Gremlin inquired, sounding astounded by the very notion.

Lynx grinned and nodded vigorously. "Bingo. What a great idea, huh?"

"You're pulling our legs, no?" Gremlin wanted to know.

"I'm serious. Just think of how terrific it would be to get away from the Home for a while. What better way to put a little spice into our life?"

"What better way to wind up dead?" Ferret rejoined.

"A trip away from the Home would break the monotony, alleviate our boredom," Lynx maintained.

"But *you're* the only who who is bored," Ferret stated.

"Does this mean you don't like my idea?"

"Like it? I think it's the craziest, stupidest, most feeble-witted, insipid, blockheaded idea you've ever had, and that's saying a lot."

"Does that mean no?"

"*No!*" Ferret shouted, practically exploding.

Lynx studied his irate friend for several seconds. "I expected you to act this way."

"You did?"

"Sure. You're a pessimist."

"At least I'm a *live* pessimist."

"There ain't no need for you to make up your mind today. Think about the idea for a while. You'll come around to my way of thinking," Lynx predicted.

"Now there's a scary thought, yes?" Gremlin interjected.

"Lynx, there's no way I'll ever agree to this asinine plan of yours," Ferret stated. "I let you talk me into becoming a Warrior against my better judgment, but I'm not giving in this time. We have a good life at the Home. The Family treats us with respect and has accepted us as members, and in return we use our hybrid abilities to protect those who have been so kind to us. We do our fair share of work, and we face our fair share of danger. There's no reason to rock the boat by demanding to be taken on the next run. Gremlin and I aren't bored, and we want to leave well enough alone."

"Party poopers."

"Besides, how can you want to travel far from the Home when you have Melody?" Ferret asked.

"She won't object if I go on a run."

"Of course she won't. She loves you too much to stand in your way. For her sake you should think twice about your idiotic ideas," Ferret said. "You have the most to lose, and you can cause the woman who loves you tremendous grief. Think about how lucky you are, Lynx. You're the only one of us who has a mate, a woman endowed with feline attributes exactly like yours. You're the only one who has someone to go home to when your work is done for the day. Do you know how much Gremlin and I envy you? Do you know how badly we wish we had a mate of our own?"

Lynx averted his gaze and pretended to be interested in a nearby oak tree. "It's not fair bringing Melody into this."

"You were the one who made an issue of fairness," Ferret countered. "How fair are you being to Melody if you're willing

to desert her for weeks at a stretch just because you're bored
with your job?''

''The other married Warriors leave their wives when they
go off on missions,'' Lynx said defensively.

''Yes, they do. But I don't know one wife who's happy about
the arrangement. They recognize the necessity but they resent
being separated from their loved ones. Take Blade and Jenny
as an example. He leads every mission. He's away from the
Home more than anyone else, and his prolonged absences have
upset Jenny immensely. Do you want to do the same thing to
Melody?''

''You should never hurt the one you love, no,'' Gremlin
commented. He gazed at the azure sky, anxious to resume their
search, thinking of his close friend, Blade. Then he glanced at
a patch of weeds to his left.

''We could always take Melody with us,'' Lynx suggested.

''Are you out of your mind? You'd imperil her life by taking
her into the Outlands?''

''She can handle herself. And she's always sayin' how she'd
like to get out of the cabin more often.''

''Excuse me, yes?'' Gremlin said, but the other two ignored
him.

Ferret gestured angrily at Lynx. ''You're amazing! Do you
know that? Just when you come up with the dumbest idea in
the history of this planet, just when I think you can't possibly
top your previous stupidity, you outdo yourself! Now you want
to take Melody on a mission. The Doktor must have given you
a lobotomy when no one else was looking.''

''This is important, no?'' Gremlin stated.

''Butt out,'' Lynx snapped, glaring at Ferret. ''What Melody
and I decide to do with our lives is our business. If she wants
to go on a mission, it's fine with me.''

''Well I'm not going, and that's final!''

''Who needs you? Stay at the Home and hide in your shell.
Let life pass you by.''

''Stop arguing, yes?'' Gremlin urged, to no avail.

''It would serve you right if Melody kicked you out the door,''

Ferret said to Lynx.

"You'd just love that, wouldn't you?"

"No."

"And why not?" Lynx demanded, his voice rising.

"Because if she gives you the boot, you'll probably end up bunking with us."

"And I suppose you're too good to share a room with me?"

"It's not the sharing I mind. It's the fact that you snore like an erupting volcano."

"Says who?"

"Says me!"

Gremlin stepped between them, grinning happily. "I'm sorry to interrupt your friendly conversation, but this is most important, no?"

"What the hell is it?" Lynx asked.

"We must return to the Home immediately, yes?" Gremlin informed them.

"Why?" Ferret asked.

For an answer, Gremlin extended his right arm and opened his hand.

"Damn!" Lynx exclaimed.

"What are we waiting for?" Ferret asked.

Off they raced toward the Home.

Chapter Five

Who was this woman?

Floating on the threshold of consciousness, Berwin saw a lovely woman running toward him, a radiant vision with blonde hair and green eyes, her body clothed in a shimmering silver gown. He seemed to be standing at one end of a grass-covered field. She approached him from the other end, sprinting with the fleetness of a doe, her arms outstretched in his direction, her mouth moving, forming the same word over and over and over again.

Berwin couldn't hear her.

He took several strides, his head cocked to one side, but the mysterious woman was still too far away. "Who are you?" he shouted. "What do you want?"

The blonde kept coming, kept mouthing the word.

Berwin trembled as an intense feeling that he should know her swept through him. Strangely, although the word she spoke wasn't audible, although at least 50 yards separated them, her features were incredibly clear. He could see every detail: her full lips, her rounded cheeks, and the panic in her eyes, as if she were afraid she wouldn't reach him in time.

"What is it?" Berwin called out.

She opened her mouth wide to reply, and suddenly the entire scene dissolved into shards of light. She abruptly disintegrated into glowing bits and pieces.

"No!" Berwin cried, and a black fog enshrouded his mind. Fear gripped him, an inexplicable fear out of all proportion to the content of his dream. "No!" he cried again.

And woke up.

Berwin sat bolt upright in bed, momentarily disconcerted, sweat caking his skin. He gulped and blinked a few times, wondering why the blonde woman had disturbed him so, and wished he could identify her.

"Are you all right?"

Berwin looked at the door, ill at ease at the sight of Nurse Krittenbauer standing in the doorway. "Fine," he mumbled.

The nurse walked over to the bed and placed her right palm on his forehead. "You don't have a fever. What's wrong? I heard you yell."

"I had a bad dream," he replied.

"What about?"

Berwin licked his lips and sighed. "It was nothing, really."

"You let me be the judge," Krittenbauer said. "Tell me about your dream."

Reluctantly, self-conscious while relating the account, Berwin complied, concluding with, "So you can see it was no big deal."

"Perhaps," she said ambiguously. "Did you have any other dreams?"

Bertwin shook his head. "Not that I recall. All I took was a short nap. I dozed off while waiting for Doctor Milton to return with my family."

"Your parents and your sister will be here soon," Nancy informed him.

"Good," Berwin said, excited at the prospect.

"And from now on I want you to fill me in on every dream you have."

"What? Why?"

"So I can note them for the doctor."

"But why? How important can my dreams be?" Berwin asked.

"They can be very important. They might provide the key to unlocking your memory. They might enable us to help you in dealing with the trauma of your accident," Krittenbauer said.

"I had no idea," Berwin responded. "Okay. From now on I'll let you know about every dream."

Nurse Krittenbauer smiled. "Fair enough. Is there anything you'd like before your family arrives?"

"Any chance of getting a set of clothes?" Berwin inquired. "This hospital gown is drafty."

"Your folks are bringing clothes for you, I believe."

"Do they know about my amnesia?"

She nodded. "Doctor Milton told them."

"How'd they take the news?"

"I don't know. I wasn't there," Krittenbauer said, and studied him for a few seconds. "You seem nervous about meeting them."

"Wouldn't you be?" Berwin asked. "They're my family, but I don't remember a thing about them. Not one solitary fact. They'll be like strangers to me."

"They're nice people. You'll like them."

"Will they like me?"

"What a ridiculous question. Of course they will," she replied. "And seeing them will be great therapy."

"I hope you're right," Berwin said nervously.

Nurse Krittenbauer stepped to the door. "Why don't you try to relax while I check on the doctor and your family."

"I'll try."

She smiled and departed.

Berwin rested his head on the pillow and stared at the ceiling. If he was lucky, maybe the shock of meeting his family would jolt him into recalling his past. He desperately wanted to remember, especially the beautiful blonde woman he'd seen in his dream. Somehow—call it intuition, a sixth sense, or whatever—he knew the woman existed. She wasn't merely a figment of his imagination. He felt compelled to identify her. A frown creased his lips at the thought of the upcoming days, weeks, months, even years, he might have to wrestle with the enigma of his existence. Who *was* he, deep, deep down?

A light knock sounded on the door and in walked Doctor Milton, grinning congenially. "Hello, Mister Berwin."

Berwin sat up, his gaze on the doorway. "Where's my family?"

"Waiting in the corridor," Doctor Milton said as he came over.

"Bring them in," Berwin prompted.

"In a minute. Are you ready to meet them?"

"I've never been more ready for anything in my life," Berwin assured him.

"Really? Well, I'd advise you to prepare yourself for the worst. I don't mean to dash your hopes, but I've seen enough cases like yours to know how the typical patient reacts. I imagine that right about now you're on pins and needles."

"You don't know the half of it."

Doctor Milton put his right hand on the giant's shoulder. "Then allow me to submit some unsolicited advice. Don't permit your expectations to soar too high. You may remember events in your past when you see your family. You may not. There's no guarantee.

"I realize that."

"Good. Do you also realize how much of a strain this will be on your family? Remember, they haven't talked to you in three months. And they're extremely upset about the amnesia. They'll probably be awkward and nervous. Don't hold it against them."

"I won't," Berwin promised.

Doctor Milton nodded, appraising his patient carefully. "Okay. Then I guess you're as ready as you'll ever be." he turned toward the door. "Nurse Krittenbauer, you can bring them in now."

Berwin leaned forward expectantly, his abdomen tied in knots. He glued his gaze to the doorway and held his breath, his hands clenched at his sides.

Into the room came three people.

First to enter was a tall, gray-haired man dressed in a blue shirt and brown pants. His eyes were blue, his nose thin, his features ruggedly handsome. He strode directly to the bed and reached for Berwin. "Son! Son! At last!"

Although his initial reaction was to recoil and push the man away, Berwin let himself be hugged, trying hard to cover his disappointment. He hadn't recognized his own father! It was as if a total stranger embraced him. Over his father's left shoulder, he studied the two women who were coming toward him.

In the lead was a stocky woman in her sixties. She wore a light green dress and held a black purse in his left hand. Streaks of gray accented her otherwise-sandy hair. Her cheeks and jaw were both fleshy. Tears welled in her green eyes the instant she saw him. "Son! You're with us again!"

Berwin's father moved aside so his mother could hug him, and Berwin felt her wet tears on his cheek as she pressed her face to his and kissed him.

"Oh, son!"

"Mom? Dad?" Berwin said, his forehead furrowing in mounting chagrin. He didn't know his mother either!

"Bobby?" interjected the second woman. She appeared to be a few years younger than Berwin. Blonde hair fell almost to the small of her back. Her athletic form was clad in a red blouse and black slacks.

"Sis?" Berwin responded, and for a fleeting second he experienced a stirring within him, as if he was about to recall something important. But the moment passed, leaving him with the blank slate he called a mind, and he almost pounded on the bed in anger.

"Do you recognize me, Bobby?" his sister asked.

"Bobby?"

His mother clasped her right hand to her mouth in astonishment. "Oh, no!"

"You don't know your own name?" his father inquired in a dazed tone.

"I knew my name was Berwin," the giant said, and winced at their pained expressions.

"Bobby, it's me, Trish," said his sister. She came closer and tenderly touched his cheek, her blue eyes reflecting her concern. "Don't you remember me?"

Berwin looked from one to the other, then stared at the foot of the bed, his broad shoulders sagging. "I'm sorry. No. I don't remember any of you."

His mother started bawling, and his father took her into his arms to comfort her.

"I warned you this might happen," Doctor Milton interjected. "Don't take it personally."

"Why should we do that?" Trish responded, her tone making the very idea sound ridiculous.

"You never know," Doctor Milton said. "I once saw a mother who got mad at her daughter because the daughter couldn't remember her."

"We'd never get mad at our Bobby," the mother managed to say between sobs.

Berwin gazed at them. "I'm truly sorry. The last thing in the world I'd want to do is cause you any grief."

"It's okay, Bobby," Trish said. "We understand." She gave his left hand a squeeze. "The doctor told us you'll need time to recover. But knowing you have amnesia doesn't lessen the shock, you know?"

"Tell me about it," Berwin said.

Trish laughed. "At least you haven't lost your sense of humor."

The father cleared his throat. "Son, I want you to know that we're behind you one hundred persent. We'll stick by your side until this ordeal is over. Don't worry about your medical expenses. The insurance will cover everything."

"Who cares about insurance at a time like this?" Trish declared testily.

Berwin's father shrugged. "It's always nice to know."

Trish glanced at the physician. "How soon can Bobby come home with us?"

"That will depend on his progress. His release will be at my discretion."

"Wouldn't his memory return faster if he was in familiar surroundings?" Trish persisted.

"As I told your brother a few minutes ago, there are no guarantees. The amnesia will simply have to take its course," Doctor Milton said.

"Terrific," Trish muttered. She sat down on the edge of the bed and smiled at Berwin. "You must feel uncomfortable as hell."

"Trish! Your language!" the mother said primly.

"I'm sure everyone here has heard the word before," Trish replied.

Berwin grinned, despite himself. Even though he didn't recognize his sister, there was a quality about her he liked, a certain toughness he found highly admirable. She vaguely resembled the blonde woman in his dream, and he wondered if the dream had simply depicted her differently.

"Can we take Bobby for a walk?" the father asked Milton.

"Not today, I'm afraid," the physician replied.

"When?" Trish inquired.

"Perhaps in two or three days. Remember, he's been in a coma for three months. Your brother might look fit as the proverbial fiddle, but we don't want to push him. We don't want him to overstep his limits before we ascertain exactly what his limits are," Doctor Milton said.

Trish glanced at Berwin. "Sorry, bro. Looks like you're chained to your bed for a while."

Berwin grinned and shrugged. "After three months, what's a few more days?"

His mother took a white handkerchief from her purse and dabbed at her moist eyes. "Would you like us to bring books, magazines, and newspapers on our next visit? You've always been an avid reader."

"Yeah," added his father. "I always thought you'd become a college professor, not involved in construction."

"You know Bobby likes to work outdoors," Trish said.

"What do you like to do?" Berwin asked her.

"Me? Oh, I like to date hunks. I like seafood, and I adore skiing."

"You're not married?"

Trish chuckled. "Not yet, thank goodness. I haven't met the man yet worth giving up my freedom for."

A thought occurred to Berwin and he did a double take. "I never thought to ask. Am I married?"

"No," Trish responded. "You were once, but she left you."

"What was her name?"

Trish glanced at Doctor Milton, who nodded. "Her name was Crystal."

"Where is she now?"

"Who knows? Who the hell cares?" Trish replied. "She and you split up about four years ago. I never did care for her. Too snooty for my tastes. Good riddance, I say."

Berwin stared into her eyes. "Did we have any children?"

"Nope. You wanted to have kids but she didn't."

Berwin digested the information, aware of being the focus of attention for everyone in the room. "Describe Crystal for me."

"She's got blonde hair, like me," Trish said. "Her eyes are green, I think. She's attractive, if you like her type." She deliberately emphasized the last word distastefully.

The description matched the woman in his dream, Berwin realized. So he'd been dreaming about his former wife. It was strange, though, that he hadn't experienced any lingering resentment or hostility toward her. Wouldn't such a reaction be normal if his wife had ditched him?

If?

Berwin grinned. There he went again, venting his unfounded suspicions. Why couldn't he just accept what everyone told him at face value?

"What's so funny?" Trish asked.

"Nothing," Berwin said, shaking his head. "How long can you stay today? I want to hear all about myself."

"We'll stay until they shoo us out," his mother said.

Doctor Milton stepped forward. "Uhhhh, I hate to nip this meeting in the bud, but you'll only be able to remain for another minute or two," he informed them.

"What?" Trish responded angrily. "Why can't we hang around for a few hours, at least?"

"Because I don't want to unduly stress your brother," Doctor Milton said. "I warned you earlier that the reunion would have to be brief."

"But I'm fine," Berwin said. "They don't have to go."

"Yes, they do," the physician insisted.

"What about tomorrow?" the mother inquired.

"Tomorrow afternoon you can visit for an hour."

"That's all?"

"Sorry," Doctor Milton said. He nodded at the nurse.

Berwin's father sighed and placed his right hand on Berwin's shoulder. "We'd stay if we could. You understand that?"

The giant nodded.

"This isn't fair," his mother remarked bitterly.

"Life isn't fair, Mom," Trish said.

Nurse Krittenbauer stood near the door. She motioned at the doorway and frowned. "I'm sorry, folks, but you'll have to leave now. Doctor's orders."

"Wait for me out in the hallway," Doctor Milton requested.

The father, mother, and daughter each hugged Berwin, promised him they would be back the next day, and departed.

"How do you feel?" Doctor Milton asked when they were gone.

"I don't remember any of them," Berwin answered sadly.

"Don't expect a miracle," Doctor Milton said. "We have our work cut out for us before your memory returns."

Berwin slumped onto the bed.

"I do have some good news for you," Milton mentioned.

"What?" Berwin responded, sounding totally disinterested.

"Your parents brought some of your own clothes for you to wear. The clothes will be kept at the nurse's station overnight, and tomorrow morning you can put them on."

"Thanks," Berwin mumbled.

"Are you going to mope all night?"

"Maybe."

"A positive attitude does wonders for the disposition and promotes healing," Doctor Milton stated. "If you succumb to the doldrums, if you let the amnesia get the better of you, you'll delay your recovery."

"I'll try to cheer up," Berwin said.

"Hang in there," Doctor Milton advised, and walked into the corridor. He saw the others standing at the junction and he hurried to them, grinning triumphantly.

"Did he fall for our act?" Trish asked.

"Hook, line, and sinker," Milton told them.

"Our superiors will be very pleased," the mother commented.

"Let's not become overconfident," the father advised. "Don't forget who we're dealing with."

"A few more days and we might have the information. Then we can end this charade," Milton said.

"What will they do with him after they get the information?" Krittenbauer inquired.

"What do you think?" Trish replied, and snickered.

Doctor Milton glanced back at the giant's room. "I certainly wouldn't want to be in his shoes."

Chapter Six

He was crouched on a low, stout limb six feet above the narrow game trail, his leg and thigh muscles coiled to spring, a black machete held in each hand. His brown eyes locked on the ten-point buck approaching from the west and he froze.

The buck paused and sniffed the cool morning air uncertainly, displaying the innate caution that had enabled the animal to reach full maturity in a land overrun with predators. It studied the sprawling maple tree directly ahead, then gazed at the small pond 20 feet beyond the tree. Thirst compelled it to move forward, its keen ears straining to detect the presence of flesh-eaters.

Poised and ready, the man in the tree waited patiently, seemingly sculpted from stone. His black hair had been cropped into a crew cut. His eyebrows, nose, and lips were all thin, lending a hard, almost cruel aspect to his countenance. A short-sleeved brown khaki shirt, brown pants, and brown leather boots, all crafted to fit by the Family Weavers, covered his six-foot-tall frame. In addition to the matched machetes, he had a pair of SIG/SAUER P226's around his slim waist, one auto pistol in a flapped holster on each hip.

A robin winged by overhead, and the buck paused to idly observe the bird.

The man remained immobile.

With a bob of its antlers the buck came on, ambling ever nearer to the pond. Many times the white-tailed deer had quenched its thirst at that drinking hole, and not once had danger been present.

This day would be different.

The man in the tree noted every step the buck took. He felt no particular pleasure at what he was about to do. Despite their characteristic wariness, deer seldom bothered to look up into the trees for a lurking threat because they were rarely attacked from above. So the routine kill he was about to make did not pose any challenge to his finely honed skills. It was a simple matter of slaying game to put meat on tables at the Home.

Unaware of the man's proximity, the buck walked under the spreading limbs of the maple.

In a fluid, graceful motion the man pounced, dropping from the limb and angling his descent to land on the ground next to the buck's right front shoulder. The machetes streaked through the air, unerringly on target.

The white-tailed deer could do no more than snort in surprise as the human alighted besided it. Instantly it went to bound away, its four legs beginning to propel it upwards. But before the buck completed the leap, its right front leg was sliced off at the knee, causing it to stumble forward with blood gushing from the stump.

With ambidextrous precision the man swung both machetes, cutting off the right rear leg and slashing open the buck's neck simultaneously. He straightened and stepped back, expressing no emotion as the dear toppled to the ground and kicked and thrashed on the grass. Crimson drops spattered in every direction. Wide-eyed in terror, the buck gradually weakened, its efforts feebler and feebler.

The man in brown wiped his machetes clean on the grass, then reached up and slid them into the crisscrossed black canvas

sheaths attached to his back. A black handle jutted above each
shoulder, within easy grasp at a moment's notice. He folded
his wiry arms and watched the buck's death throes. Only when
he was satisfied that the animal had expired did he crouch and
flip the deer onto its back.

A pool of blood had formed underneath the buck.

He wiped excess blood from the buck with his left hand, then
proceeded to slowly lift the white-tail's front half. Squatting
and twisting his torso, he managed to drape the heavy carcass
on his back. Then, grunting from the exertion, he rose to his
full height with the buck across his shoulders.

In the surrounding forest life went on. Birds sang and insects
droned.

The man hiked southeastward, skirting the southern rim of
the pond, his tread measured, his stride indicating he could walk
for hours with his burden and not tire. The terrain being
generally flat, he made good time. Within an hour he spotted
the 20-foot-high brick walls enclosing the 30-acre survivalist
retreat built over a century ago by the man who started the
Family, Kurt Carpenter.

Situated in northwestern Minnesota, on the outskirts of the
former Lake Bronson State Park, the compound had been
stratagically positioned by the Founder to enable the Warriors
on the ramparts to see anyone or anything approaching from
all directions. As added insurance, the ground for 150 yards
in every direction had been cleared of all trees, brush, and
boulders. Consequently, the Warrior on the west wall spied the
man in brown and gave a shout for the drawbridge in the center
of the wall to be lowered.

The man crossed the field, watching the drawbridge lower
slowly. He glanced at the Warrior on duty on the rampart and
recognized the tall, lanky figure and distinctive red Mohawk
of Ares, the head of Omega Triad.

"Hello, Marcus," Ares called down.

"Hi," Marcus responded. He stepped onto the drawbridge
and paused at the sight of the person awaiting him on the
opposite bank of the inner moat. Mystified, he advanced until

he was two yards from the man and halted. "Hickok," he said in greeting.

The Family's preeminent gunfighter nodded, his thumbs looped in his gunbelt, his gaze roving over the buck. "Howdy, Marcus. Where'd you bag the deer?"

"At that pond northwest of here," Marcus replied.

"Isn't baggin' game a job for the Hunters?"

Marcus studied the gunman for a moment. "Usually. But Blade has always permitted the Warriors to go after game when we're not on duty."

"True, but you're supposed to let Blade know first."

"Blade's not here," Marcus noted.

"Which means *I'm* in charge," Hickok said. "Why didn't you let me know?"

Marcus went to shrug, but the weight of the buck prevented him. "I didn't think you'd mind."

The gunman stepped closer, smiled, and leaned forward, his nose an inch from Marcus's. "*I mind,*" he stated emphatically, then straightened. "I expect to be treated with the same respect you'd show Blade. When you're off duty, your time is your own. But if you want to go traipsin' off into the woods, you're supposed to let the head Warrior know. What if something had happened to you out there? We wouldn't have had the slightest idea where to search for your mangy hide."

"Nothing would have happened," Marcus responded.

"Oh? Are you an Empath, now, too?"

"No—" Marcus began.

"Are you invincible?"

"No, but—"

"Do you have cow patties for brains?"

Marcus opened his mouth to reply.

"If you *ever* pull a stunt like this again, I'll have you up in front of a Review Board so fast you'll be dizzy," Hickok snapped, his tone low and hard. "Savvy?"

"I understand," Marcus said, "but—"

"There are no buts about it," Hickok declared. "And Blade will hear about this when he gets back."

"Do we know where he is?" Marcus asked hopefully.

"We have a good idea where he's at," Hickok disclosed. "The hybrids found a clue."

"Are you going after him?"

"Yep. Geronimo is comin' with me. We'll take the SEAL."

"Are you sure the two of you will be enough?" Marcus asked.

"Nope. I'm aimin' to take along one other Warrior," Hickok said, and grinned.

"Who?" Marcus inquired, and suddenly, in a flash of insight, he understood why the gunman had been waiting for him. "Me?"

"You," Hickok confirmed.

"But why me?" Marcus blurted out, astounded by the unexpected development.

"Why not?" Hickok rejoined.

"I've never been on a run before," Marcus noted.

"All the more reason you should go on this one," Hickok said. "You're one of the youngest Warriors. You're—what?— twenty-four?"

Marcus nodded.

"Well, no offense meant, but you're also one of the least experienced. Most of the other Warriors have been on missions away from the Home. I reckon it's about time you had a turn."

"Ares hasn't been on a run yet," Marcus mentioned absently, excitement mounting inside him. Here was his chance to venture into the Outlands! Here was an opportunity to test the skills he'd so diligently honed! He realized Hickok had selected him for that very reason, to give him the combat experience he needed, and his respect for the gunman rose several degrees.

"Omega Triad is on wall duty. Ares will be on duty for six more hours, and we're leavin' in thirty minutes. Geronimo is loadin' our gear and supplies into the SEAL right now," Hickok said.

Marcus gazed at the compound, at the dozens of Family members engaged in various activities, at children playing and adults conversing and a Musician playing a guitar, and he suppressed an urge to shout for joy. "There are other Warriors who haven't been on runs," he noted, too thrilled to think of anything else to say.

"Yeah, I know," Hickok replied. "Teucer, Samson, Spartacus, and the mutants ain't been on runs. They'll get their turn sooner or later." He paused and chuckled. "Actually, I was fixin' to take Yama. But Lynx spoke up and reminded me that there are Warriors who haven't gone out on the SEAL yet. He had a good point. I was up past midnight decidin' who to take." He beamed. "Lucky you."

"Maybe Lynx was hoping you'd take him."

"You could be right," Hickok said. "When I bumped into Lynx an hour ago and told him I'd picked you, he walked away muttering something about meatheads."

"What all should I bring along?" Marcus asked.

"Pack a couple of changes of clothes. Go to the armory and grab as much ammo as you can carry. And you'll need an automatic rifle or a machine gun."

"I prefer my machetes."

Hickok glanced at the machete handles protruding above Marcus's shoulders. "I've been meanin' to ask you. Why'd you choose those pigstickers as your favorite weapons, anyway?"

"I know all about your interest in the American Old West," Marcus mentioned. "That's why you carry the Pythons, dress in buckskins, and talk weird."

"Who the blazes claims I talk weird?" Hickok demanded.

"Everybody."

"Oh. Just so it's unanimous."

Marcus grinned. "With your interest in the Old West, I know you can appreciate my interest in the ancient gladiators. I've read every book in our library on the customs of the Romans. I know all about the contests they staged in huge arenas, pitting the gladiators against other fighters or wild beasts."

"Yeah. I know. I read about 'em in school," Hickok said. "But takin' on a hungry, slobberin' lion armed with just a dinky fishnet and an oversized fork seemed like a dumb way to make a living. I know Spartacus is partial to that era."

"He is," Marcus stated. "And since he became a Warrior

before I did, he had first dibs on the only broadsword the Founder stocked in our armory. The same with Ares. He took the only shortsword. The Founder collected an extensive sword and knife collection, but he rarely included more than one of each type of sword. Rikki-Tikki-Tavi got the only katana.''

"Leavin' you with the machetes.''

"Exactly. Oh, there are a few different swords left, but I like the machetes the best. They're lightweight and razor sharp.''

"Give me a one-hundred-and-fifty-eight-grain hollow point over a flimsy piece of metal any day,'' the gunman quipped.

"Who will be in charge of the Warriors while you're gone?''

"Rikki will hold down the fort.''

"And who will fill in for me? My Triad will be one short,'' Marcus observed.

"Don't worry. You're covered. I've already made the arrangements. The other Warriors will take turns filling in for you.''

Marcus stared at the field to the west of the compound. "I can hardly wait.''

"Then get your tail in gear. Pack your clothes, grab an automatic from the armory, and meet me at the SEAL in twenty minutes,'' Hickok directed.

"On my way,'' Marcus said, and took a step. He paused and glanced at the gunman. "Wait a minute. You haven't told me where we're going.''

"Beantown.''

"Where?''

"Didn't you pay attention in history class?''

Marcus shook his head. "Except for the Greek and Roman periods, history bored me to tears.''

"I spent the past half hour in the library readin' up on the city we're headin' to. Beantown is another name for Boston, Massachusetts. The nickname has something to do with Boston baked beans, whatever the blazes they are.''

"Blade is in Boston?''

"That's that we figure,'' Hickok said. He reached into his

right front pocket. "The hybrids found this late yesterday afternoon. The Elders spent all night in a conference, and they voted to send a rescue team to Boston. Plato agreed with them."

Marcus knit his brows in contemplation. If Plato, the wise Family Leader, believed the evidence warranted a trip to Boston, warranted traveling half the distance of the continental United States through the Outlands, then the clue the mutants found must be important and clear-cut.

"Here it is," Hickok said, and held out his right hand.

Marcus stared at the object in the gunman's palm for several seconds, perplexed. "That's it? A pack of matches?"

"Read the matchbook cover."

Marcus used his left hand to raise the matchbook to eye level so he could read the red lettering on the cover, part of which had been torn off. Several letters in the first word were missing.

—ERS. SAM'S BAR. NOW AND FOREVER. BOSTON, MASS.

"Why do you look as if you just swallowed a frog?" Hickok asked.

Marcus wagged the matchbook. "This is the big clue? How do we know there's a connection between this and Blade?"

"Several reasons. First, the matchbook is in tiptop shape, except for the teensy tear, which means it wasn't lyin' around exposed to the elements for very long. Second, the furballs and Gremlin found it on the trail they were following between the field where the helicopter landed and the spot where Blade was jumped. Third, there ain't too many folks from Boston waltzin' around the countryside."

"So the Elders think that one of those who captured Blade must have dropped the matchbook?"

"You're a regular Pinkerton detective."

"A what?"

"Never mind."

"I take it that Boston wasn't hit by a nuclear weapon during the war?" Marcus inquired.

"Not as far as we know. Boston is in Commie territory," Hickok said.

"The Russians took Blade?"

"Looks that way," Hickok answered harshly. "We have a score to settle with those vermin. So get packin'."

Marcus nodded and hurried off.

"Hold it," Hickok said.

"What?" Marcus replied, halting in midstride to look back.

"Aren't you forgettin' something?"

"Like what?"

Hickok pointed at the dead deer. "You'll look sort of silly waltzin' around the Home with a buck on your shoulders. You might want to ditch it before you start packin'."

Marcus glanced at the deer and grinned sheepishly. "Damn, I was so excited, I almost forgot about it." He hastened off.

The gunfighter waited until Marcus was beyond hearing range, then threw back his head and laughed. Terrific! he told himself. Just what he needed on the run. A wet-nosed whippersnapper. He ought to have his head examined for deciding to take an inexperienced Warrior along. Even with the best of intentions, Marcus could well get them all killed.

Chapter Seven

Berwin was eating a late breakfast consisting of oatmeal and toast when Doctor Milton entered his room.

"Good morning," the physician declared. "How are you feeling today?"

"Better. I had a good night's sleep," Berwin replied. He took a bite of toast and chewed hungrily.

"I left instructions for you to be allowed to sleep as late as you liked," Milton said, coming to the edge of the bed. In his right hand he held a small notebook and a pen.

"Thanks," Berwin said, and took a swallow of milk. "And thanks for letting me have the oatmeal. I was afraid I'd have to eat pea soup."

"Pea soup is for lunch," Doctor Milton informed him.

"I can hardly wait."

Milton grinned. "Did you have any dreams last night?"

"A few."

"What about?"

Berwin shrugged. "Nothing important."

"You let me be the judge of that," the physician said.

"Then Nurse Krittenbauer was right? My dreams are important?"

"Extremely important," Doctor Milton verified. "I want you to tell me every detail you can remember."

"Right this minute?"

"Right now," Milton stated. "Leave nothing out, no matter how trifling you think it might be."

Berwin straightened and scratched his forehead. "Let's see. I can remember two dreams. The first one was shorter."

"What was the subject?"

"Myself as a small boy, I think," Berwin said. "I was about five or six years old and big for my age."

Doctor Milton began taking notes. "And what were you doing in this dream?"

"Nothing. Just standing there with the saddest expression you can possibly imagine. Strange, huh?"

"Not really," Milton said. "The dream state often lacks coherence. Did you speak in the dream?"

"No."

"Not a word?"

"No," Berwin reiterated. "Why? Are the words I say in my dreams crucial?"

"They could be, yes," Doctor Milton answered.

"Well, I didn't say a word in either dream."

"Tell me about the second one."

Berwin leaned back, fingering the last piece of toast on his tray. "The second dream was definitely bizarre. I seemed to be floating in the air above a huge, walled fortress or compound. It was daytime, and there were a lot of people moving about. Four brick walls enclosed the fortress, and in the middle of the west wall was some kind of bridge, possibly a drawbridge."

"Yes. Go on," Doctor Milton prompted, writing as fast as he could.

"Along the inner base of the walls ran a stream, forming a moat—"

"Where did the stream originate?" Doctor Milton asked, breaking in. "Was there an underground spring in the compound?''

Berwin pondered for 30 seconds. "No. As I recall, the stream entered the fortress under the walls at the northwest corner, then was diverted to run along the base of all the walls."

"Did the stream flow out of the compound at any point?"

"The southeast corner."

"Very interesting," Doctor Milton said. "Please continue."

Berwin concentrated, idly tapping his fingers on his food tray. "There were six enormous structures located in the western section of the compound. I also saw a row or two of cabins in the central area, arranged in a line from north to south."

"What about the enormous structures? Can you tell me more about them?"

"They were square in shape. My guess is they were concrete buildings."

"How were they arranged? In a line like the cabins?"

"No. They were spaced about one hundred yards apart and arranged in the shape of a triangle."

"What else?"

"That's all I can remember," Berwin said.

"There must be more," Milton insisted. "What did you see in the eastern section of the compound? What were the concrete buildings used for? Were there any apparent weaknesses in their defenses? Any machine guns mounted on the walls? Any cannons?"

"Weaknesses in the defenses?" Berwin repeated quizzically. "Machine guns on the walls? Are we discussing a dream or a plan of attack?" he joked.

Doctor Milton did a double take and tensed for a moment, then laughed and lowered the notebook to his side. "Sorry. I got carried away. I know that any trivial detail might help us restore your memory, so I was pushing a little too hard."

"I understand," Berwin said.

"Did you feel as if you knew the place you saw in your dream?" the physicain queried.

"I felt as if I should. When I woke up this morning, its name was on the tip of my tongue," Berwin divulged. "But the feeling didn't last very long.''

"Most unfortunate," Milton commented.

"What does it all mean?"

"I require time to analyze your dreams before I can tender an opinion.''

Berwin sighed and spooned oatmeal into his mouth.

"After your breakfast you can wash up. Then Nurse Krittenbauer will bring your clothes.''

"I finally get out of this flimsy gown?"

Milton nodded and walked to the doorway. "I'll return in a few hours to conduct several tests. Behave yourself until then. Don't wander off without permission."

"I won't," Berwin pledged. He frowned and nibbled on the toast. Another day in bed did not appeal to him in the least. If the doctor wouldn't permit him to walk around, then perhaps a little harmless exploring was in order.

"See you later," the physician said, and departed.

Berwin finished his breakfast while ruminating on the possible significance of the compound he'd observed in his dream. The place had seemed so real. All of his dreams the past two days had been exceptionally realistic, and he wondered why. He hoped Milton's analysis would aid in restoring his memory.

Nurse Krittenbauer arrived with a basin of hot water, a washcloth, and a towel. "Ready for your sponge bath?"

"As ready as I'll ever be."

"Do you want me to do the honors?" she asked with a mischievous wink.

"I can manage," Berwin said.

"What a spoilsport," Nancy cracked. She exchanged the basin for the meal tray and left.

The giant slid out of the bed and gave himself a sponge bath. As he finished he glanced at the window and decided to open it to let fresh air in. He dropped the cloth in the plastic basin and stepped around the head of his bed. How strange, he thought. The images outside were blurred and distorted by the glass. He leaned on the sill and examined the pane. Although the window appeared to be normal glass from even a few feet away, close up the glass displayed a prismlike effect. No one inside could see out.

Was it deliberate? And if so, why?

Berwin inspected the edges for a latch, surprised to discover there was no way to open the window. What reason could they have for sealing the window frame?

"What are you doing?"

Berwin pivoted and saw Krittenbauer in the doorway with an armful of clothes. "What's with the window?"

"Were you planning to jump?" she asked in jest, walking over to the bed.

"Don't be ridiculous."

"This is a hospital, Mister Berwin. Some of our patients are emotionally distraught. Some have attempted to commit suicide. To remove temptation and prevent anyone from jumping, all of the windows above ground level can't be opened. You're on the sixth floor."

"Oh," Berwin said, moving toward her. "But why can't I see outside?"

The nurse grinned. "What a bundle of curiosity you are. The windows have been constructed so no one can see out because we don't want our patients spending all their time looking outside when they're supposed to be in bed."

"Are you referring to me?"

"Is there anyone else in this room?"

Berwin sat on the edge of the bed. "Are those my clothes?"

"Yes," Nurse Krittenbauer said, and deposited the pile next to him. "The doctor says you can wear your own clothes, but if I catch you out of bed again without permission I'll confiscate them and you'll wear a hospital gown until the day you leave."

Berwin chuckled. "Was that a threat?"

"That was a promise." She turned on her heels and exited.

The clothes turned out to be a flannel shirt, jeans, black socks, and brown leather boots. He stripped off the gown and donned the flannel shirt first. The material fit tightly across his shoulders and upper arms, too constricting for comfort. He buttoned the shirt and experimented, raising and lowering his arms, puzzled.

How could he have worn the shirt on a regular basis when it
hampered his movements? The pants weren't much better. They
threatened to burst at the seams if he bent over too far. He had
better luck with the socks, but the boots were too narrow at
the tip for his toes to fit comfortably.

Berwin went to the mirror and scrutinized his appearance.
If his own family hadn't delivered the clothing, he'd suspect
that the clothes weren't really his.

A soft noise, a shuffling, came from behind him.

Turning, Berwin found a skinny man dressed in brown
overalls and a brown cap, a broom in his left hand. The man
appeared to be startled to encounter someone in the room.
"Hello," Berwin said.

"Hello," the man responded uncertainly, scrutinizing
Berwin's attire. "I didn't think anyone was here."

"May I help you?" Berwin asked, coming around the foot
of the bed.

The man shook his head vigorously, apparently intimidated
by Berwin's size. "No, thanks. I'm the day-shift janitor."

"What's your name?"

"Jennings. Tom Jennings."

"Bob Berwin. Please to meet you," Berwin said, and offered
his right hand.

Jennings stared at the hand for a bit, then shook gingerly.
"Do you work here too?" he inquired.

"Yeah," Berwin joked. "I'm the resident amnesiac."

"You're a resident?" Jennings queried in surprise. "Man,
let me give you a word of advice. Don't let Doc Milton or old
iron-guts Krittenbauer catch you dressed in those duds. They'll
skin you alive. They like all their men resident-types to dress
in white."

"But they gave me permission to wear these clothes," Berwin
said.

"They did?" Jennings questioned. "Then you must be a
hotshot at whatever the hell amnesiacs is and they're givin' you
special treatment."

Berwin suddenly perceived that the janitor had misunderstood his remark about being the resident amnesiac, and he was about to correct the man's misconception when Jennings made a most curious comment.

"They usually have a fit if a resident walks around in civvies. They're military all the way." He walked to the far corner and started sweeping the floor.

"Military?" Berwin repeated.

Jennings glanced at the giant. "Don't get me wrong, Doctor Berwin. I ain't got nothin' against you military types. I'm just not used to all the spit and polish, is all."

"Isn't spit and polish what hospitals are all about?"

Jennings snorted. "Now there's a good one. It might as well be,' seein' as how the HGP runs this floor and keeps close tabs on the whole hospital. A mouse can't get into Khrushchev Memorial without permission."

"Don't you mean Kennedy Memorial?" Berwin asked.

The janitor laughed. "You're a real funny guy, Doc. This place ain't been called that in eighty or ninety years."

Lines formed on Berwin's forehead as he tried to comprehend the janitor's revelations. Nothing made sense. He needed more information, but if he asked the wrong question, if he disclosed his ignorance, the man might clam up. "How long have you worked here?" he inquired.

"Oh, about fifteen years," Jennings said, sweeping under the bed. "Before that I pushed a broom at the Committee for State Security building over on Proudhon Avenue." He paused and swallowed. "I don't mind tellin' you that workin' there gave me the creeps."

"Why?"

Jennings looked up. "Would *you* be comfortable workin' in the KGB building?"

"I guess not," Berwin said, playing along, scheming to elicit more news. "You must enjoy working here better."

"You bet your ass I do," Jennings stated. "I don't have to work nights any more, which makes my wife happy. And some days, when they have a patient on this floor, I get to go home early."

"Why's that?"

"You haven't been workin' with the HGP very long, have you? They're a hush-hush bunch. When they've got patients on this floor, the guard at the desk tells me not to worry about cleanin'. They take care of it themselves, but they don't do as good a job as me."

The guard at the desk? Berwin shook his head in bewilderment, feeling as if his world had been turned topsy-turvy.

"Yes, sir," Jennings went on, still sweeping. "They do a half-assed job, and I have to work harder when they finally give me the green light. But I don't mind if it gets me a few extra hours off now and then. You know what I mean?"

"I think so," Berwin replied.

"So what's the field you're in again? Amnesiactics?" the talkative janitor inquired absently.

"It has to do with the mind."

"Really? I heard the HGP was more into bodies."

"Oh?"

"Yeah. You know. The gene thing. I never did understand science much."

A tack he could take occurred to Berwin, and he promptly took advantage of the opening. "You must hear a lot about our work."

"Oh, the usual scuttlebutt," Jennings said, sweeping nearer to the door.

Berwin stepped aside so the janitor could pass him. "Like what?" he asked, willing himself to remain calm, keeping his tone level and casual.

"There was talk about all the experiments being done on this floor," Jennings said. "They say the experiments were classified Top Secret. I even heard the North American Central Committee are the bigwigs runnin' the show."

Berwin rubbed his forehead, utterly confused. He couldn't recall his own past, but the name Khrushchev, the letters KGB, and the North American Central Committee all sparked a flicker of recognition in the vague reservoir of his memory, and the word he associated with all three filled him with apprehension:

Russians. Why did the thought of Russians provoke such anxiety? What did he know about them? Think! he admonished himself. The Communists in Russia had been the mortal enemies of the United States, hadn't they? But how could there be Russians in Boston? Doctor Milton had told him the United States won World War Three. He looked at Jennings, who was sweeping with his back to the doorway, and went to ask another question.

Before he could, a pair of hands clamped on the janitor's shoulders and Jennings was hauled roughly from the room.

Chapter Eight

"Where the blazes are we?" Hickok asked, his hands gripping the steering wheel firmly, his eyes on the rutted, pothole-dotted road directly ahead.

"You're doing the driving," the stocky man across from him responded. "Don't you know?"

"I know we're in Iowa," Hickok said.

"The white man's sense of direction never ceases to amaze me," cracked his traveling companion.

"And the cantankerousness of Injuns never fails to get my goat."

"Cantankerousness? Wow. I'm impressed. I didn't think you had words larger than two syllables in your vocabulary."

Hickok sighed and glanced to his right at the man he considered his virtual brother, one of the two best friends he had, the other one being Blade. "Look, Geronimo, will you quit givin' me a hard time and take a gander at the map in your lap?"

"I can't," Geronimo responded. A green shirt, green pants, and moccasins covered his muscular form. His black hair was cut short, barely covering his ears. The Blackfoot heritage in his family was evident in his facial features. Under his right arm in a shoulder holster rested an Arminius .357 Magnum, and tucked under the front of his brown leather belt and slanted across his right hip was a genuine tomahawk, taken from the enormous collection of weapons stockpiled in the Family armory.

"Why the heck not?" Hickok demanded.

Geronimo looked at the gunman, his brown eyes twinkling. "Because I want to keep my eyes on you and the road."

"Why? I'm doing a right smart job."

"That's a matter of opinion."

"We haven't had an accident yet, have we?" Hickok queried, wrenching on the wheel to avoid a hole two feet in diameter situated in the middle of the highway.

Geronimo clutched the dashboard for support, swaying as the transport lurched to the left. "No, but we still have about a thousand miles to cover. I'm sure you'll find something to hit."

"Thanks for the vote of confidence, pard," Hickok muttered straightening the steering wheel, pleased at the vehicle's superb response.

The Solar Energized Amphibious or Land Recreational Vehicle, dubbed the SEAL by the Founder, had been one of Kurt Carpenter's pet projects. He'd wisely foreseen that his descendants would require a unique vehicle capable of traversing the radically altered post-apocalypse terrain, and he had invested millions to have the SEAL developed according to his rigorous specifications.

Vanlike in shape, the transport was a revolutionary prototype powered by the sun. A pair of solar panels attached to the roof collected the sunlight, which was then converted and stored in special batteries housed in a lead-lined casing underneath the SEAL. The body was constructed of a heat-resistant, shatter-proof plastic, fabricated to be nearly indestructible and tinted green. The tint prevented anyone outside from viewing the occupants. Four puncture-proof tires, each four feet high and two feet wide, supported the transport.

Knowing his followers would need protection from the hordes of scavengers, raiders, and worse roaming the countryside, Kurt Carpenter had hired mercenaries to add armaments to the SEAL. They'd done their job well. A flamethrower with an effective range of 20 feet had been mounted in the center of the front fender, surrounded by layers of flame-retardant insulation. Hidden in the front grill was a rocket-launcher, and concealed in recessed compartments under each headlight was a 50-caliber machine gun. A surface-to-air missile, heat-seeking with a range of ten miles, perched on the roof above the driver's seat. All four weapons were activated by toggle switches on the dash.

Carpenter hadn't spared any expense on the interior either. Spacious and comfortable to alleviate the strain of extended trips, a pair of bucket seats at the front accommodated the driver and a passenger. Between the seats ran a small console. Behind them, running the width of the vehicle, was another seat for passengers. The rear section served as the storage area for their supplies, spare parts, tools, and whatever other provisions were needed.

From the person sitting in the wide seat came a request. "I'd like to know where we're at too, Geronimo. Would you check for me?"

"For you, Marcus, yes," Geronimo replied, and consulted the map spread open on his thighs.

Hickok shighed. "This is going to be a *long* trip."

"I can't believe we've gone hundreds of miles and haven't run into trouble yet," Marcus commented.

"You sound disappointed," Geronimo said, tracing his left forefinger on the map, following the route they'd taken.

"I was hoping to see some action," Marcus stated. "I've heard so many stories about how dangerous the Outlands can be, but this run so far has been boring with a capital B."

"Count your blessings," Geronimo responded.

"Don't you want to see action?" Marcus asked, sounding surprised.

"The less I see, the better."

"But why? We're Warriors, aren't we? Fighting is our

business, right?''

"Yeah. But I hope to live long enough to enjoy my grand-children.''

"Not me," Marcus said. "I don't care if I live to be thirty. I'm not married, like you guys, and I don't have any children. All I live for is to do my duty as perfectly as possible. And I can think of no greater honor than to go out in the line of duty, to die in the service of our Family.''

Hickok glanced back at the man in brown. "Listen up, eager beaver. I didn't bring you along so you could become a martyr. You're not allowed to kick the bucket without my say-so. Savvy?''

"I'll do my best to stay alive," Marcus said. "Don't get me wrong. I don't have a death wish.''

"Here we are," Geronimo declared, leaning over the map. "We're on Highway Three, or what's left of it, a few miles west of a tiny town called Strawberry Point.''

"The folks livin' before the war sure gave their places strange names," Hickok remarked.

"Maybe they grew a lot of strawberries," Geronimo guessed.

Marcus sat forward and leaned on the console. "Why are we sticking to the back roads? Wouldn't we make faster time if we used the major highways?''

Geronimo shook his head. "Blade started the practice of using only the secondary roads and avoiding all the larger towns and cities. From past experience we know that the major highways are patrolled by bands of scavengers who ambush everyone they meet, and the cities are swarming with all kinds of misfits and mutations. We're better off sticking to the back roads. Hickok knows what he's doing," he said, then placed his left hand over his mouth and mumbled, "Oops.''

"I heard that!" Hickok declared. He grinned and looked at Geronimo. "You finally admitted it.''

"Admitted what?''

"Don't play innocent with me, pard. You finally admitted I know what I'm doing. And I've got a witness.''

"Would you believe it was a slip of the tongue?''

"Nope.''

"Can I plead temporary insanity?"

"Nope. I've got you dead to rights. You actually paid me a compliment."

"I pay you compliments all the time."

"Oh, yeah? Like when?"

Geronimo winked at Marcus, then gazed at the gunman. "Like the time Sherry claimed you are the most aggravating man on the planet and she couldn't understand why she loved a dimwit like you."

"My missus said that?"

Geronimo nodded. "Yep. She also said you were becoming more aggravating every day."

"So how'd you compliment me?" Hickok asked suspiciously.

"I told her it wasn't humanly possible for you to become more aggravating than you already were."

"Gee. Thanks," Hickok muttered. He stared at the vegetation lining both sides of the road, then gazed out the windshield as the SEAL crested a low hill. The sight he saw made him tramp on the brake, sending the transport into a slide, slewing the front end at an angle. With an abrupt jerk the vehicle lurched to a stop.

"What the—!" Geronimo exclaimed, both his hands on the dashboard. "See what I mean about your driving."

Hickok nodded straight ahead. "Looks like Marcus will get his wish."

Geronimo faced front and scowled.

Forty yards from the SEAL, stacked ten feet high and arranged in a pile stretching from the woods on the north side to the woods on the south, completely blocking Highway Three, was a stack of recently fallen trees, the leaves still green and healthy.

"Blast!" Hickok snapped. "There's no way around unless we cut through the forest, and that'd slow us down."

"Is this an ambush?" Marcus inquired excitedly.

"This is an ambush," Hickok confirmed.

"All right!"

"Try not to get too broken up about it," Hickok quipped, studying the layout, his right hand tapping on the steering wheel.

"How will we handle this?" Marcus questioned.

"I'm thinkin'," Hickok said.

Geronimo sniffed loudly. "I thought I smelled something burning."

"Pass out the long guns," Hickok directed Marcus.

The man in brown twisted and reached into the rear section, where two automatic weapons and a rifle lay on top of the supplies. He grabbed the rifle first, a Navy Arms Henry Carbine in 44-40 caliber, and passed the weapon to Hickok.

"Thanks," the gunman said.

Next Marcus gave an FNC Auto Rifle to Geronimo. Then he seized the Heckler and Koch Model KH 94 he'd selected from the many automatics available in the armory, and cradled it in his arms. Once a semiautomatic, the HK 94 had been converted to full-auto capability by the Family Gunsmiths, whose job it was to insure every weapon in the armory worked properly.

"We could use a rocket or the flamethrower on the barricade," Geronimo suggested.

"I want to save the rockets and the incendiary fuel for later. We might need 'em," Hickok said.

"How about if we ram it?" Marcus proposed.

Both Hickok and Geronimo glanced at the man in brown and slowly shook their heads.

"Why not?" Marcus asked.

"For all we know, there could be explosives planted in there," Hickok noted. "If we ram it, we might be blown to kingdom come. It's not likely, I'll admit, but we can't take the chance. The SEAL is tough, but dynamite or a grenade would damage it."

"We have to push those trees aside," Geronimo stated.

Hickok nodded. "The SEAL could do it. Someone has to go out there and check those trees before we try, though." He frowned. "I'll go."

"You can't go," Geronimo said. "We can't risk anything happening to you. You've had the most experience driving the SEAL. I'll go."

"Let me go," Marcus interjected, but neither of his fellow

Warriors paid attention.

Hickok looked at Geronimo. "You know they'll be waiting for you."

"I know," Geronimo said.

"Let me go check," Marcus said.

"I want you to stay here," the gunman told Marcus.

"Give me one good reason."

"I said so."

"That's not good enough," Marcus stated testily. "I have just as much right as Geronimo does to go out there."

"Geronimo has more experience," Hickok said.

"So? Didn't you bring me along on this run so I could get experience for myself?"

"I reckon I did."

"How am I supposed to get the experience I need if you keep me cooped up in the SEAL?"

"You can watch us."

"Come on, Hickok," Marcus urged. "I don't need a baby-sitter. Let me prove I'm reliable."

Annoyed, Hickok gazed at the barricade. Marcus had a point. The man deserved a chance to show how good he was. "Okay. I'll compromise. Both of you will go. I'll cover you with the SEAL."

"Try not to run us over," Geronimo said, and opened his door.

"Try not to get your butt shot off," Hickok said.

Geronimo grinned. "I didn't know you cared."

"I don't. I just don't want you to lose whatever it is you use for brains."

With the utmost caution Geronimo slid to the pitted, cracked asphalt. He crouched below the door, scanning the barricade and the woods, his entire body tense.

Marcus climbed between the bucket seats and went to follow Geronimo.

"Be careful," Hickok said.

"I won't let you down," Marcus replied. "I'm not a kid, Hickok. I don't need a mother hen watching over me all the time."

"I know that or I wouldn't have brought you along," the gunman stated. "And if you ever call me a mother hen again, I'll shoot your toes off." He smiled sweetly.

Marcus gripped the HK 94 and jumped to the ground beside Geronimo, who promptly swung the door shut. The muted whine of the SEAL's engine seemed extraordinarily loud to Marcus.

"You take the left side. I'll take the right," Geronimo instructed him.

Together they straightened and stepped around the front of the transport, then advanced slowly toward the barricade, their automatic rifles leveled, their eyes alertly probing the vegetation.

An unnatural stillness pervaded the forest. Nothing moved, not even an insect. The birds were hushed.

Marcus walked along the left side of the highway, his body tingling with expectation. He licked his dry lips and willed himself to stay calm. If his excitement got the better of him, he'd become careless. He prided himself on his ability to remain cool and collected at all times, even in the direst crisis, and here was a golden opportunity to put his self-control to the ultimate test. Hickok would stop treating him as a brainless novice if he proved his dependability.

Wait!

What was he doing?

Marcus almost stopped, startled by the realization he was *thinking*. He was letting his mind be distracted by internal musing when he should be totally focused on the external situation. Peeved at his lack of discipline, he made his mind a blank, sublimating his conscious thought, concentrating on the road, the barricade, and the woods. The road, the barricade, and the woods. The road, the barricade, and—

Something moved in the woods.

Marcus continued to advance, pretending he hadn't noticed the movement, his finger caressing the trigger of the HK 94. He glanced at Geronimo, who appeared to be unaware of the movement in the trees. From the rear came the sound of the

SEAL's huge tires crunching on the asphalt as Hickok followed them.

A twig snapped off to the left.

Marcus gazed at the barricade, now 20 yards distant. The tangled branches jutting from the downed trees formed an ideal curtain of green for any enemies who might be lying in concealment. Even as he watched, one of the limbs quivered, its leaves fluttering, as if someone had bumped it. For a second he felt exposed and vulnerable, knowing that he was the proverbial sitting duck, but he shook off the feeling and stepped forward.

Ten more yards were covered without incident.

Marcus glanced at Geronimo, who still seemed to be oblivious to the ambushers; he was walking along nonchalantly instead of being wary, which astounded Marcus. He knew Geronimo was rated as one of the best Warriors, and he couldn't comprehend why the Indian wasn't more concerned about the trap. Unless, he reasoned, Geronimo's attitude was a ruse, a method of lulling their adversaries into complacency, a means of allowing the Warriors to get closer to the barricade without drawing fire.

Another limb shook for a moment, then subsided.

Five yards separated the Warriors from the fallen trees.

And suddenly a dozen forms rose from hiding at the barricade, while from the forest on both sides of the road poured 30 or 40 shrieking, bloodthirsty figures.

Chapter Nine

"What the hell do you think you're doing?"

Berwin stepped quickly to the doorway and saw Jennings in Doctor Milton's grasp. The kindly physician's features were contorted in fury, and he was shaking the janitor violently.

"Answer me, damn you!" Milton barked.

Jennings's eyes were wide, his face a mask of terror. The broom had dropped to the floor. "Sweeping!" he replied fearfully. "I was just sweeping!"

"We don't require your services today, you dolt!" Milton hissed. "Who gave you permission?" He suddenly became aware of Berwin's presence and immediately added, "Don't say a word yet. We'll get to the bottom of this shortly." With a visible effort he composed his raging emotions and released the janitor. "Pick up your broom."

Jennings promptly obeyed.

"Is there a problem?" Berwin asked. "The man was just cleaning my room."

Doctor Milton cleared his throat and studied the giant's countenance. "Was that all?"

"What do you mean?" Berwin responded, intentionally sounding puzzled by the question.

"This is a special floor. When we have patients such as yourself, our nurses attend to the cleaning chores. We don't want our patients inadvertently disturbed. The janitors are only permitted on this floor when we don't have patients," Milton explained.

Berwin shrugged. "No harm done."

"Did he talk to you?" Milton inquired.

"We chatted a bit," Berwin said, and he saw Jennings gulp and blanch.

"What about?" Milton questioned gruffly.

"Oh, about how he likes working days instead of nights, and about how he likes this job much better than whatever his last one was," Berwin answered with an air of innocence.

"That was all?"

"He mentioned how happy his wife is," Berwin said. He almost grinned at the relieved expression on the janitor.

"Nothing else?" Milton pressed him.

"That was it," Berwin responded. "I wasn't upset by the conversatiaon at all."

The physician glanced at Jennings, then at Berwin. "Okay. You're right, of course. No harm has been done. I apologize for flying off the handle, but you must appreciate my position. Many of my patients are undergoing delicate treatment, and the most innocuous comment could jeopardize my therapy by triggering a relapse."

"I understand," Berwin assured him.

"Good. Then why don't you wait in your room while I escort Mister Jennings from the ward?"

"Fine," Berwin said, and moved to the bed. He mentally counted to ten, then darted to the doorway and peered out.

Doctor Milton and Jennings were just going around a corner down the corridor to the right. He checked to insure the hallway was empty, then dashed after them, padding to within five feet of the junction, where he halted with his back to the wall. From past the corner came an angry voice, Milton's.

"—in a cell and throw away the key! You stupid son of a bitch! You could have ruined all our work!"

"I didn't do nothin'!" Jennings replied timidly. "Honest, Colonel. It wasn't my fault."

"Then whose is it?"

"The guard's."

"Hey, asshole, don't blame me," a new voice interjected, evidently the guard's.

"You waved me on," Jennings said.

"Like hell I did," the guard snapped.

"Tell me what happened," Milton ordered.

Berwin listened intently, his eyes roving up and down the corridor.

"I got off the elevator and saw the guard talkin' to Nurse Schmidt at the desk," Jennings detailed. "I said 'Janitor,' and he gave a little wave of his hand, like I was supposed to do the cleaning today."

"Bull!" the guard declared. "I waved you off. You were supposed to get back in the elevator and leave."

"Didn't you notice him walk by you?" Milton asked, an edge to his tone.

Berwin heard the guard cough.

"No, sir."

"Why not?" Milton inquired harshly.

"I assumed he'd get back on the elevator and leave," the guard said.

"You *assumed*?" Milton repeated.

"Yes, sir. Jennings should've known we have a patient on the floor," the guard commented.

Milton's voice became acidic. "And exactly how the hell was he to know that? By reading your pathetic excuse for a mind?"

The guard said nothing.

"Don't blame Jennings for your incompetence," Milton stated. "You were flirting with Schmidt when he arrived, and you didn't pay any attention to him whatsoever. Instead of verbally instructing him to leave, as required by regulations, you waved your hand to send him on his way. Am I right?"

"I didn't just wave. I motioned with my whole arm," the gurad said defensively, then added, almost as an afterthought, "sir."

"Is that right?" Milton asked again.

A female voice, unfamiliar to Berwin, answered.

"I wasn't paying much attention, sir."

"Why not, Nurse Schmidt?"

"I was talking to Private Crane."

Berwin heard Milton hiss.

"Both of you can consider yourselves on report."

"But sir—" Private Crane said, starting to object.

"Silence!" Milton ordered. "You may mistakenly believe that just because you are temporarily assigned to the HGP, and because this is primarily a biological-research project, that you can afford to goof off at your job. You're about to learn the hard way that such is not the case. I will personally report this breach of security to the general."

"You wouldn't, sir!" the guard exclaimed, clearly horrified at the likelihood.

"You've brought this on yourself, Crane," Milton said.

"What about me, Doc?" Jennings threw in. "Are you going to report me too?" His voice wavered as he spoke.

"Don't worry, Jennings. This wasn't your fault. There won't be any repercussions against you."

"Thank you, Doc," Jennings said, the words dripping with relief.

Berwin cocked his head, his attention aroused by a peculiar droning noise punctuated by a tickling sound similar to the ringing of a small bell.

"What's going on here?" inquired a new voice.

Berwin straightened, recognizing the new arrival as Nurse Krittenbauer.

"Ahhh, Nancy. You won't believe what has happened," Milton said.

"Try me."

Deciding that he'd risked detection long enough, Berwin hurried to his room. Once on his bed he sat with his forehead in his hands and pondered the quagmire of deception in which he was embroiled. Nothing was as it seemed. No one was who they claimed to be. Fact and fabrication were tangled indiscriminately.

Dear Spirit! What had he gotten into?

Who *was* he?

He tried to sort the truth from the falsehoods, beginning with the simplest deduction, counting them off in his head. One, if he really was in Boston, Massachusetts, then Boston must be controlled by the Russians. Two, if the Russians were in control, then the United States had lost the war. Three, he was in a special ward administered by Russian doctors and scientists who were involved in a highly classified project. Four, Milton might actually be a physician but he was also a colonel, which indicated a military connection. Five, and predicated on his observation about Milton, Nurse Krittenbauer must be more than a nurse, perhaps another officer, if the respectful tone Milton had used toward her signified she was a peer. If so, Krittenbauer must be a plant assigned to watch him closely under the guise of being a nurse. Six, and most disturbing of all, he must figure prominently in whatever project the Russians were conducting.

Berwin frowned and closed his eyes. He still didn't know why he instinctively viewed the Russians as his enemies. Think! he wanted to shout. Think!

And suddenly distinct memories flooded his mind in a torrent. He remembered World War Three and its aftermath.

World War Three had transpired 106 years ago, and neither side had emerged unscathed. The Soviets launched a two-pronged attack against the continental United States with conventional forces after their initial nuclear strike at a few strategically selected targets. Contrary to the media-fostered popular misconception, the Russians weren't interested in destroying America; they wanted to *conquer* the country. The Soviets wanted America's natural resources, and turning the U.S. into a devastated radioactive wasteland would have defeated their purposes. Thermonuclear devices were used on certain military installations and a few major cities, such as New

York and San Diego. But the Russians employed neutron bombs more extensively because the neutron variety were far less destructive and produced far less fallout.

On the Western Front the Soviets launched a massive drive through Alaska and Canada, aimed at the Pacific Northwest. Their armored columns were stopped in British Columbia by the worst winter in Canadian history, and they were forced to retreat back onto Russian soil.

The attack on the Eastern Seaboard was eminently successful. They wrested control of a corridor stretching from the Atlantic Ocean to the Mississippi River, including New England, southern New York, southern Pennsylvania, Maryland, New Jersey, southern Ohio, southern Indiana, and portions of Illinois, Kentucky, Virginia, and West Virginia. They also conquered sections of North and South Carolina. Eventually the Russian drive sputtered as resistance mounted and they experienced shortages of men and supplies.

For 70 years the Russian forces in American maintained their domination over the belt of occupied territories, receiving infrequent shiploads of supplies from the motherland. Then, all contact with the Soviet Union ceased. The shortwave and crypto-graphic communications from Russia stopped. All ships sent to investigate were ever heard from again. The reason wasn't a mystery.

The Soviet regime, weakened by the staggering cost of the war, both in terms of personnel and armaments, and beset at home by ever worsening shortages of the simple necessities, eventually succumbed to internal pressures brought to bear by the non-Russian peoples and the virulent ethnic minorities who had always resented Russian dominance. Many rose up in rebellion and toppled their Communists oppressors.

Leaving the Russians in America stranded.

Realizing that without reinforcements from the motherland their numbers would gradually dwindle until the subjugated Americans were tempted to revolt, the Russian leaders in the U.S. opted to establish an ingenious alternate system for replenishing their ranks. They began a system of modified racial breeding. Carefully selected American women were forcibly impregnated, and their children were raised by the State. The offspring were educated, trained, and indoctrinated by the occupation government. Communism was exalted. Russian values and history were stressed. The system produced soldiers every bit as Russian and as devoted to Communism as if they had been born and raised in the U.S.S.R. All of them were fluent in Russian and English.

Berwin opened his eyes and stared at the wall, feeling oddly happy despite his predicament. At last his memory was starting to return! Now if he could only recall who the hell he was, he'd be delirious! Although he knew more than he did before, he still didn't know what the Russians were up to at the hospital, and he had no idea how he fitted into the scheme of things.

So what should he do?

Stay where he was and try to uncover the Russian project? Or should he escape from the hospital? If he did, where would he go?

Damn.

What a mess.

Footsteps sounded outside and Nurse Krittenbauer entered, all smiles. "Hi. How are you feeling?"

Berwin pasted a welcoming grin on his face. "Fine, thanks."

"I heard you had a visitor," she commented, coming over to the bed.

"Yeah. A janitor came in here and swept the floor. Doctor Milton didn't seem very pleased."

Krittenbauer scrutinized his face intently. "Did he explain the reason to you?"

Berwin nodded. "He was concerned about his patients."

"What all did the janitor and you talk about?" Krittenbauer inquired casually.

"Not much."

"Like what, specifically?" she prompted.

"Oh, he talked about his job and his wife. Nothing unusual. Why?"

Krittenbauer shrugged. "Just asking."

"So what's on the agenda today?" Berwin asked, her. "Do I get to go outdoors?"

"Not yet, I'm afraid. But your family will be back to visit you later, so you shouldn't be too bored."

"I can hardly wait," Berwin said, feigning enthusiasm.

"Can I get you anything?"

"How about explosives so I can blow a hole in the wall and a six-story-high ladder so I can climb down and escape this boredom?" Berwin proposed.

Nurse Krittenbauer laughed. "Sorry. But you're stuck here for the duration."

Berwin sighed. "That's what I'm afraid of."

Chapter Ten

In the millisecond before Marcus squeezed the trigger, he heard Geronimo cut loose with the FNC and knew the Indian's nonchalance had been a sham. He saw six of the forms at the barricade topple over, then added a withering burst from the HK 94, downing four more. He instantly dove for the asphalt as the figures closing in from both sides opened up. Bullets buzzed overhead and thudded into the road. Without a break in his motion, he rolled to the left, presenting as difficult a target as possible, swiveling and aiming at the attackers surging from the woods on his side of the highway. He aimed and fired on the move, and he was gratified to see three foes drop—and then he knew what they were.

The dozens of ambushers charging from the forest and manning the barricade were scavengers, a large band of predatory wanderers who preyed upon everyone they encountered. Scavengers were the bane of the postwar era, as prolific as the large rats that inhabited the underground sewers and tunnels in the cities. The Outlands were infested with both.

Marcus shot two more, continuing to roll, never lying still

for a second. To do so would mean his death.

Shabbily attired, many in filthy rags, and armed with everything from pitchforks to lever-action rifles, the scavengers screamed and bellowed as they rushed the two Warriors.

Geronimo and Marcus were taking a fierce toll of their adversaries, but the Warriors were hopelessly outnumbered. The fleetest scavengers were almost to Highway Three. In mere moments Geronimo and Marcus would be overwhelmed.

The heavy thundering of the SEAL's 50-caliber machine guns rent the air, rising above the general din. A lethal hail of rounds punched into the scavengers on the barricade, mowing them down, and the whine of the transport's engine increased sharply in volume as Hickok floored the accelerator and drove the vehicle directly at the obstruction.

The majority of the scavengers turned their attention to the SEAL, peppering its impervious shell with bullets, arrows, and even spears, all of which were deflected.

Briefly free of attackers, Marcus risked a glance at the transport and saw it 15 feet away and barreling forward. He expected the gunman to ram the barricade, but the brakes were abruptly applied at the last possible second and the SEAL screeched to a halt between Marcus and Geronimo.

The driver's door was flung wide. "Get in!" Hickok shouted, then lunged at the passenger door.

Marcus pushed himself to his knees, about to bound to the SEAL, when he heard the thump of onrushing boots to his rear and whirled.

A tall man in jeans and a T-shirt, armed with a tire iron, was two strides off.

Marcus tried to bring the HK 94 into play, but the scavenger swung the tire iron, clipping the barrel and sending the Heckler and Koch flying. Another blow hissed at Marcus's head, and he duck and threw himself to the right. He rolled and began to rise, his right hand gripping the machete that jutted above his right shoulder, and he was still in a crouch when the machete came clear of its sheath and he whipped the blade across the scavenger's abdomen, slicing through the T-shirt and into the soft flesh underneath, cutting the man open with the same ease he would cut a melon, disemboweling his adversary.

The man shrieked, released the tire iron, and clutched at his stomach as his intestines oozed forth.

Marcus snapped his arms in an arc, sinking the machete into the scavenger's neck, nearly decapitating the man. He didn't bother to watch the scavenger fall. Instead he turned to the SEAL and took a stride.

Another scavenger, a woman armed with a makeshift metal lance, bore down on him from the right, hatred distorting her features, dressed in ragged jeans and a blue blouse. "You killed George!" she cried.

Twisting, Marcus raised the machete to block the tip of the lance, batting the six-foot spear aside. The woman's momentum carried her to within six inches of the Warrior, and he spun, reversing his hold on the hilt, and used a reverse thrust to impale the scavenger's midriff, burying the machete all the way.

The woman screeched, blood spurting from her mouth, and doubled over, the lance falling from her suddenly limp fingers.

Marcus wrenched the machete free and tried once again to reach the shelter of the SEAL.

A hefty man wielding an ax charged him.

Automatically Marcus adopted a defensive posture, elevating the machete to counter the anticipated swipe of the axe. But before the axe could descend, a .357 Magnum boomed and an expertly aimed bullet bored through the center of the scavenger's forehead and burst out the rear of the man's cranium, spraying brains, flesh, hair, and blood on the roadway. Marcus glanced at the transport.

Hickok sat in the driver's seat, a Python in his left hand. "Will you quit playin' around!" he ordered. "Get in here!"

The rest of the scavengers were converging on the SEAL with all the primal savagery of a rabid dog pack.

Marcus darted to the vehicle and clambered inside.

"About time," Geronimo quipped, already sitting in the other bucket seat, his door closed and locked.

"I lost the HK 94," Marcus informed them as he slid into the wide seat.

"Forget it," Hickok responded, about to holster the Colt and close his door when a grungy scavenger materialized outside with a rifle in his hands, which he tried to point at the gunfighter. Hickok shot the man in the head, the impact flinging the scavenger backwards.

Several rounds smacked into the windshield.

Using just two fingers, Hickok snatched at the door handle and slammed the door shut. He slid the Python into its holster and took hold of the wheel. "Hang on!"

Marcus nearly lost his balance when the gunman shifted into reverse and tromped on the accelerator, sending the SEAL racing rearward. Several scavengers were right behind the transport, and their bodies made loud thumping noises as the SEAL bowled them over.

The rest of the scavengers discharged a concerted volley.

"Mangy cow chips," Hickok muttered, braking the SEAL 30 feet from the barricade. Over a dozen scavengers were charging toward the front of the transport. He flicked the silver toggle activating the 50-caliber machine guns again, and in less than five seconds every scavenger in front of the SEAL was dead or dying, their grimy forms perforated repeatedly, pouring blood from their multiple wounds.

"Hickok!" Geronimo abruptly yelled. "The barricade!"

The gunman glanced at the wall of trees, his steely blue eyes narrowing at the sight of a lean scavenger astride the top of the barricade. *The man held a bazooka!*

"He's going to fire!" Geronimo warned.

Hickok's right hand streaked to the toggle switch marked with an R, and the next moment the SEAL lurched violently as the miniature rocket flashed from its hidden compartment in the middle of the front grill.

If Marcus had blinked, he would have missed it.

The rocket sped straight into the center of the barricade and exploded with tremendous force. A mighty explosion consumed the wall of trees and a spectacular fireball rose 50 feet skyward. Dust and debris swirled into the air, obscuring the scene in a billowing cloud.

"Wow!" was all Marcus could think of to say.

The Warriors waited for the cloud to disperse. They glimpsed scavengers retreating into the trees, and only a few desultory shots were fired in parting at the SEAL.

"Why didn't they use the bazooka on us before?" Marcus asked, leaning forward to peer out the windshield.

"The vermin likely wanted to take the SEAL intact," Hickok responded. "When we proved too hot to handle, they figured they'd blow us to smithereens."

"That band won't be ambushing travelers for a while," Geronimo commented.

"Too bad we couldn't wipe 'em all out," Hickok said.

The dust cloud rapidly dissipated. Bodies and bits of bodies were everywhere, intermixed with jagged lengths of busted logs, broken branches, and fluttering leaves.

"I thought you wanted to save the rocket," Geronimo mentioned.

Hickok shrugged. "I did. But we have two more stored in the back. Besides, I wouldn't have had to use the rocket-launcher if you two bozos had been on the ball."

"Meaning what?" Geronimo queried.

"Meanin' there were only fifty or sixty of those Yahoos. You should have been able to take them out easy."

Geronimo looked at Marcus. "You'll need to excuse him. He occasionally suffers from delusions."

"Well, I'll be darned. Look at that," Hickok said.

The barricade had been totally destroyed. A few man-sized logs, broken limbs, and leaves were scattered where the wall had stood.

"Should we replace the rocket now?" Geronimo inquired.

"Nope. There might be snipers in the trees. We'll drive a few miles first," Hickok replied, and drove forward, not bothering to skirt the corpses littering the ground. The SEAL's massive tires crunched over a half dozen before the transport passed the last of the logs and leaves and headed to the east.

Marcus sat back in his seat and stared at the blood dripping from his machete. He shifted and reached into the storage section.

"What do you need?" Geronimo asked.

"A rag."

"There's one in the toolbox," Geronimo said.

"Thanks," Marcus responded. He found the toolbox, got out a fairly clean red rag, and started to wipe the blade.

Hickok looked at the self-styled gladiator. "You did real well back there. I was impressed."

"I lost the Heckler and Koch."

"You still have those pigstickers and the SIG/SAUERs. And we'll find you a machine gun or an auto rifle somewhere. I'm sure the Commies have a few they can spare."

"My performance was shabby," Marcus remarked absently, involved with cleaning the machete.

"What's with you?" Hickok questioned. "I pay you a compliment and all you do is gripe."

"I wanted to demonstrate my competence to you. Instead I lost the HK 94 and my technique was flawed."

"Your technique?" Hickok repeated.

. Marcus nodded. "I should have taken care of that first guy in one move, not two. Economy of movement is essential in combat. You know that."

"What are you, a perfectionist?" Hickok asked, partly in jest.

"Yeah," Marcus answered.

Hickok and Geronimo exchanged glances.

"Not another one," the gunman muttered.

"Who else is a perfectionist?" Marcus inquired.

"Yama, Rikki-Tikki-Tavi, and Samson to name just three," Geronimo answered.

"How are they perfectionists?"

"Yama is constantly striving to be the perfect killing machine, the consummate Warrior," Geronimo said.

Hickok snorted, his eyes on the road. "What do you expect from a guy who took his name from the Hindu King of Death?"

"And Rikki," Geronimo went on, "is constantly trying to

attain the transcendent mental and emotional state of a perfected swordmaster. Samson wants to be a spiritually perfect Warrior, the same as his Biblical namesake.''

"So what's wrong with any of that? All three of them are outstanding Warriors," Marcus noted.

"True. And any one of them would be the first to tell you that perfectionists must always be on guard against getting carried away with their quest for perfection. You'll have to watch the same tendency in yourself. There's a fine line between perfectionism and fanaticism, and you must be careful you don't cross that line and wind up useless as a Warrior."

"That'll never happen to me," Marcus confidently predicted. He finished cleaning the machete and replaced the blade in its sheath.

"Famous last words," Hickok joked.

"You're a fine one to talk," Marcus stated. "You're just as much a perfectionist as Rikki or Yama. You spend more hours practicing your markmanship than any other Warrior. Even Sundance doesn't practice as much as you do."

"Maybe I am," Hickok acknowledged, "but I don't—" he began, but abruptly stopped, tensing. "Blast!"

Marcus looked at the level expanse of highway before them. Five hundred yards distant were three vehicles approaching at a rapid clip. The trio suddenly braked to a stop and Hickok did likewise with the SEAL.

"More trouble," Geronimo said.

"Who do you think they are?" Marcus asked.

"Maybe they're the official welcoming committee from Strawberry Point, but I wouldn't count on it," Hickok stated.

"They could be friends of the scavengers," Geronimo speculated.

"Too bad we don't have another rocket in the grill," Hickok mentioned.

"Do we cut through the forest?" Geronimo inquired.

"No," Hickok replied. "I know this buggy can travel over any type of terrain, but going through the woods would slow us down. Time is of the essence. I want to reach Boston as soon as possible.''

"If time is of the essence, why didn't we wait for the next shuttle flight and take a VTOL to Boston?'' Marcus questioned.

Geronimo stared at the younger Warrior, thinking of the weekly shuttle service initiated by the Free State of California. The only Federation faction possessing functional jet aircraft, California had been the site of a summit meeting of Federation leaders at which they'd decided to use the jets to carry correspondence and passengers on a regular basis. "The next shuttle flight wasn't due for six days," he answered. "And we wouldn't have been able to commandeer the jet without the approval of the Federal Council. By the time a meeting of all the leaders could be held, another week would have elapsed.''

"There was another reason I didn't want to wait for the jet," Hickok added. "To reach Boston, the VTOL would have to fly over Russian territory. The last time one did, the Commies shot it down. Takin' the SEAL is a mite slower, but it's also a tad safer.'' He straightened, his right hand dropping to the Henry resting on the console. "Now what's this action?''

The three vehicles were slowly closing on the transport. From the passenger side of the foremost vehicle, a gray car, fluttered a white flag.

"They want to talk,'' Geronimo said.

"I don't trust 'em,'' Hickok stated.

"We should give them the benefit of the doubt,'' Geronimo suggested.

"Okay,'' Hickok responded reluctantly. "But don't doze off on me.'' He headed toward the vehicles, keeping the speedometer at ten miles an hour.

"They're armor-plated,'' Geronimo observed.

Marcus looked closer. Sure enough, each vehicle was covered with makeshift armor plating. Mesh wire had been fastened to the windshields. Two of the three were cars, the third a pickup. Riding in the bed of the pickup were three men in seedy clothes, and each man held a machine gun.

"Maybe they'll let us pass,'' Geronimo said, but his tone lacked conviction.

"If they don't, we'll have a fight on our hands," Hickok noted. "I don't like the notion of wastin' more ammo."

"We can always ram them," Marcus recommended.

The gunfighter glanced over his right shoulder. "Have you ever wanted to learn to drive the SEAL?"

Marcus grinned. "You bet I have."

"Forget it."

The distance between the transport and the three armored vehicles slowly narrowed. When only 20 yards separated them, they halted.

Hickok put the SEAL in Park. He saw a man climbing out the passenger side window of the lead vehicle, a scrawny figure carrying a Winchester. Tied to the end of the barrel was the white flag, a ragged towel. "Looks like they want to palaver."

"To what?" Marcus asked.

"Palaver is Martian for shoot the breeze," Geronimo translated.

"Oh."

"You two stay put," Hickok directed. He scooped up the Henry and opened his door.

"I should go, not you," Geronimo said.

Hickok shook his head. "I need to stretch my legs. Keep your peepers peeled. If they try any funny stuff, back my play." He eased to the asphalt.

"I'll go with you," Marcus offered.

"I told you to stay put," Hickok said. He slammed the door, hefted the Henry, and strolled toward the man bearing the white flag.

The three men in the bed of the pickup, which was parked a few yards behind and to the left of the lead car, all trained their machine guns on the Warrior.

Chapter Eleven

Berwin wanted answers.

He'd spent the better part of the past two hours contemplating the course of action he should pursue, and he'd reached the conclusion that the only way he could discover the reason for his presence in a Russian-controlled hospital in Boston would be to find an office or a file room. Any written records pertaining to his case were bound to shed light on the mystery. His parents and sister were due to arrive in several hours. Doctor Milton had departed for lunch, and Nurse Krittenbauer had told him she'd be downstairs for an hour.

He had all the time he needed.

Berwin stepped to the door, insured the corridor was empty, and bore to the right, heading for the junction. He tiptoed to the corner and listened. Someone coughed lightly and another person began humming. He eased his left eye to the edge and ventured a peek.

Twelve feet from the junction stood an obviously bored guard, a man in a blue uniform with the words ACME SECURITY printed on the cap he wore. In a black leather holster on his left hip rode a pistol sporting black grips. His brown hair had been clipped short, and his brown eyes regarded his surroundings with ill-concealed disdain. He yawned and stretched.

Not more than a yard behind the guard was an elevator shaft, the door closed and the needle on the floor indicator overhead pointing at the third floor.

Between the junction and the elevator, on the right side of the hall, positioned close to the wall, was an L-shaped counter eight feet in length and half as wide. Stationed at the counter, attired in a smart white uniform, humming to herself as she sorted through a stack of index cards, was a nurse with black hair. Positioned at the opposite end of the counter, at the open end near the elevator, was a shut door on which the word OFFICE had been imprinted in large block letters.

Berwin stared at that door, wishing he could get inside.

"I need to take a leak," the guard unexpectedly announced.

"Go ahead. I'll cover for you," the nurse said.

"Give a yell if the patients try to rebel," the guard joked, walking over to the counter.

"You'd better go to the bathroom and get back to your post," the nurse advised him. "If Milton or Krittenbauer see you talking to me, we're in hot water."

"Okay," the guard said. "We don't want to wind up like Crane and Schmidt."

"What happened to them? Why were they relieved of duty? Why were we called up here on such short notice?"

"I don't know all the facts. Apparently they slacked off and let an unauthorized person on the floor. Milton and Krittenbauer hit the roof. I was told that Krittenbauer had them relieved on the spot and ordered replacements on the double," the guard related.

The nurse lowered her voice conspiratorially. "Just between you and me, Colonel Krittenbauer scares me to death."

"Yeah. I know what you mean. The KGB has the same effect on me," the guard stated. He moved away from the counter, toward the junction. "Shout your lungs out if the elevator starts up. That's a private baby reserved for those using this floor, so it might be Kritterbauer or Milton coming back.''

"You've got it," the nurse promised.

Berwin whirled and raced swiftly and silently to his room.
He ducked inside and flattened against the door, breathing
heavily, his adrenaline pumping. Crouching, he peered out and
saw the guard walk past the junction and disappear, evidently
en route to the bathroom. Berwin straightened and returned to
the junction. He glanced to the left, elated to find the guard
nowhere in sight, then looked at the nurse's station.

Still humming, still sorting the index cards, the nurse had her
full attention focused on her task.

There would never be a more opportune moment.

Berwin sank to his hands and knees, then crawled to the
counter. He moved slowly along the base, holding his breath,
expecting to hear the nurse cry out in alarm, but he crept past
her without incident, the five-foot-high counter screening him
from her view. He came to the open end and paused, gazing
at the office, wondering how he could sneak in there unnoticed.

With a loud whirring noise the elevator began to operate.

"Oh, no!" the nurse said.

Berwin glanced at the elevator, then at the nurse. She had
turned to her left, away from the office.

"Nelson!" the nurse called out. "The elevator!"

Quickly Berwin glided to the office and tried the doorknob.
To his delight the door opened, and he hastily slid into the cool,
dark interior and closed the door quietly. Diffuse light rimmed
the border of the heavy yellow drapes covering the large window
on the far side of the room. A massive oaken desk occupied the
center of the floor. To the left, along the wall, was a sofa.
To the right, metal cabinets.

Records!

Berwin stood and angled toward the cabinets.

"The elevator is on its way up!" the nurse warned the guard.
"Hurry it up, Nelson!"

Berwin estimated he had two minutes, at the most. He reached
the file cabinets and tugged on the top drawer. Locked. In
mounting urgency, with repeated looks at the door, he attempted

to open each of the drawers. Every one was locked.

Damn.

"Come on, Nelson!" the nurse yelled.

"Don't have a heart attack," came a reply from down the hall.

Feeling supremely frustrated, Berwin attempted to open the last drawer without success. He scowled and turned toward the door.

"About time," the nurse outside said.

"I'm here, aren't I? Don't sweat it," Nelson told her, his voice growing louder with every word.

Berwin paused, confounded. He couldn't escape from the office with the guard back on duty. But what if the person riding the elevator came in? He spied a closet a few feet to the left of the metal cabinets and dashed on over.

From the corridor came the ting of a bell.

"Colonel Krittenbauer," the guard declared.

"Refer to me as Nurse Krittenbauer, you cretin," snapped a familiar voice. "What if our patient were to overhear you?"

"Sorry, ma'am," Nelson replied dutifully. "It won't ever happen again."

"See that it doesn't," Krittenbauer commanded.

Berwin opened the closet, within which he could distinguish white uniforms and other clothes hanging on a rack. On the floor were several pairs of shoes. Assorted items were piled in the corners. He secreted himself inside and drew the door to within an inch of the jamb, leaving the narrow space so he could see the room.

None too soon.

A burst of light flooded the office and Nancy Krittenbauer entered. She walked to the metal cabinets, produced a key from one of her uniform pockets, and unlocked the top drawer.

Berwin watched her flip through dozens of manila folders. She selected several and stepped to a plush chair facing the oaken desk. As she settled into the chair, Milton came in.

"You're back from lunch early," Krittenbauer commented.

"I didn't have much of an appetite," Milton replied. He closed the door, went around the desk, and sat down with a sigh.

"I didn't hear the elevator," Krittenbauer said.

"I used the stairs," Milton informed her. He placed his elbows on the desk top and supported his chin in his hands.

"Our star patient?"

"Who else?" Milton responded morosely.

"Are you upset about the possible ramifications of the incident with the janitor?" Krittenbauer inquired.

"Aren't you? If we fail, the general will bury us alive."

"You're exaggerating."

Milton sat back in his chair. "Hey, *you're* the one who mentioned firing squads, as I recall."

Krittenbauer deposited the manila folders on the edge of the desk. "So how bad can it be?"

"There are so many variable factors involved, it's difficult to make an accurate assessment," Milton said. "*If* they really talked about Jennings' work and nothing else, and *if* Jennings didn't reveal any information concerning our facility, and *if* the drug hasn't worn off prematurely, and *if* the Warrior's suspicions weren't aroused, then we *might* be in good shape."

"You don't exactly inspire confidence," Krittenbauer remarked. "Do you think Jennings blabbed?"

"He claims he didn't. But he's smart enough to realize the trouble he'd be in if we knew he divulged any details," Milton said. He smacked the desk in anger. "Damn that stupid guard! I hope the general strings Private Crane up by the balls."

"He just might," Krittenbauer stated, and smirked.

"We're so close to eliciting the information the general wants. The memories are starting to surface, just as our research demonstrated would be the case."

"Experimental drugs are notoriously unreliable. I wouldn't place a lot of faith in the Memroxin."

"We have a general sketch of the interior of the Home thanks to the Memroxin," Milton reminded her.

"But the general wants more than a mere sketch. He wants precise information, nothing less than a detailed layout of the entire compound. He wants to know the purpose for every building, and who lives in which cabin. When the HGP Unit goes in, they'll need accurate intelligence to coordinate their attack properly,'' Krittenbauer said.

"If the Memroxin doesn't wear off, we'll acquire the data the general desires."

"And then the fun part begins," Krittenbauer mentioned.

"The fun part?"

"Extracting his semen for our impregnation program should be mildly diverting. I'm certain he'll resist. The Warrior is disgustingly noble."

Berwin knit his brow in perplexity. There was that word again. Warrior. Why did he tingle every time she spoke it? He must be the Warrior to whom she referred. But what significance did the word carry? What type of Warrior was he?

"Did you know the second set of tests have confirmed the initial series?" Milton asked.

"When did you hear?" Krittenbauer responded, leaning forward.

"This morning shortly before the fiasco with the janitor," Milton said. "The written report will be on my desk by this evening. His genes appear to be virtually disease free. They rate his heritable disease quotient as almost nil."

"No wonder the general has ordered he be kept alive and unharmed at all costs. Think of the contribution he can make to future generations."

"And now you can appreciate why the general decided to use the Memroxin to extract the information. Except for the typical disorientation while the patient is under the influence of the drug, there are no known side effects," Milton said.

"Shouldn't one of us go check on our star patient?" Krittenbauer asked.

Berwin tensed. They'd discover he wasn't in his room and sound a general alarm. He had to stop them!

"I'll go," Milton offered.

"Let me. We're developing quite a rapport."

Berwin ran his hands over the floor, groping about for anything he could use as a weapon. His right hand bumped into a thin, upright object leaning in the corner, knocking it over, and the object slid to the floor, missing the clothes, making a scratching noise. Berwin pulled back from the closet door.

"What was that?" Milton asked absently.

"Did one of your lab mice escape?" Krittenbauer quipped.

"Not to my knowledge," Milton said.

Berwin heard the man rise and walk toward the closet. A fleeting panic seized him, and he clenched his fists and willed his mind to stay calm.

"I really should clean out this closet," Milton commented. "I stuff everything in here, and I never know what will fall out next."

The door swung open.

For a second both men were transfixed, Berwin huddled on the floor, coiled to spring, while Milton gaped in amazement at the giant.

"Any mice in there?" Krittenbauer joked, her view of the closet obstructed by the physician.

"Bl—" Milton started to blurt out.

And Berwin pounded with the speed of a striking cobra, his seven-foot frame surging out of the closet, his left hand clamping on Milton's throat. He stepped into the clear, holding Milton at arm's length. "Don't move!" he instructed the startled woman in the chair.

But Colonel Nancy Krittenbauer of the Soviet KGB was already in motion. She leaped erect and took two strides toward the office door, her mouth widening, about to yell for the guard.

Berwin intercepted her. He hauled Milton after him, his right arm flicking out, and his fingers locked on Krittenbauer's hair. With a brutal jerk of his right arm he whipped her backwards, causing her teeth to snap together and stifling her cry for aid, then released his hold. The power in his bulging muscles sent her sailing into the desk, her right side bearing the brunt of the impact.

Krittenbauer gasped and doubled over, her right arm pressed to her ribs. Still game, she raised her head to shout.

Berwin reached her before she could. Acting instinctively, he backhanded her across the face, the blow twisting her sideways. She tried to run but her legs buckled and she fell to her knees. "Drug me, will you?" Berwin said bitterly. He swept his right knee into her chin.

The KGB agent crumpled, unconscious.

"And now, *Doctor* Milton," Berwin stated in a gravelly tone, swinging the terrified physician around to face him, "you're going to tell me all I need to know or I'll break every bone in your body."

Milton wheezed and nodded, his hands feebly pulling on the iron vise constricting his neck.

"Now then," Berwin said, intending to begin the interrogation, but a heavy pounding on the office door interrupted him.

"Doctor Milton? Doctor Krittenbauer?" the guard called. "Is anything wrong?"

Berwin glanced at the door, his fury mounting.

Chapter Twelve

Hickok met the man bearing the white flag midway between the vehicles.

"Hey, dude. How's it hangin'," asked the other, and grinned broadly, exposing a gap where two of his upper front teeth had been. Unkempt dark hair framed his dirty face. His beady eyes, thin nose, and oval chin gave him a rodentlike aspect. He wore a green, short-sleeved shirt and jeans, both of which had seen better days decades ago. From his right ear lobe dangled a large, circular diamond-studded earring. He also sported a silver safety pin through his nose. Adorning his left forearm was a tattoo, a depiction of a sneering skull and the words HEAVY DEATH RULES.

"What the blazes are you?" Hickok responded.

The scrawny man did a double take. "Whoa. Serious hostility. What a bummer."

"What?"

"My name is Dezi."

"I'm Hickok."

"Cool name, dude," Dezi said in a friendly fashion.

"Quit callin' me 'dude,' pipsqueak," Hickok stated testily. He glanced at the three vehicles, estimating the odds. In addition to the trio in the bed of the pickup, there were two in the cab, three men in the second car, and two more in the lead vehicle, all well armed.

Dezi made a clicking sound. "Man, what did you do in your last life to deserve such a rotten karma?"

"What are you babbling about?" Hickok asked impatiently.

"Like, you're radiatin' bad vibes," Dezi said.

"And you're one marble shy of brainless," Hickok retorted. "What's with the white flag? Who are you guys and what do you want?"

Dezi held the Winchester loosely in his left hand and placed his right on his hip. "You shouldn't be rude, dude. I'm comin' to the point."

"This century?"

"We're called the Cruisers, man. We're from Motor City," Dezi disclosed.

"Where's that?"

"East of here a ways."

"I've never heard of Motor City," Hickok said.

"Oh, it was called something else before the major rumble."

"The city you're from was hit by an earthquake?"

Dezi cocked his head and cackled. "Get real, dude! I was talkin' about the war. The city was called Detroit."

"Detroit, huh?" Hickok repeated, and looked at the pickup. "You're a long way from home."

"We got tired of all the hassles, man. Tired of fightin' for a worthless piece of turf. So we split, and we've been on the road ever since."

"Doing what?"

Dezi frowned. "It's not nice to intrude on somebody's else's space, dude."

"Let me guess," Hickok said. "You're scavengers. You take whatever you want from whoever has it. How many folks have you killed? Twenty? Forty? Sixty?"

"Who keeps count?" Dezi responded, then added indignantly,

"And we're not scavengers, dude. We like to think of ourselves as road warriors. In fact, we get our kicks by wastin' crummy scavengers. There's a group of those scumbags in this area that we've hit a few times."

Hickok suddenly understood the reason for the barricade. "So you go around the countryside killin' scavengers. Women and children too, I'll bet."

"Hey, a brat grows up to be a full-grown scavenger. We do the world a favor by snuffin' them. As for the women," Dezi said, and smirked, "they're our entertainment, if you get my meaning."

"I get your drift, all right," Hickok said scornfully.

"Then let's get down to cases," Dezi proposed. He gazed past the man in buckskins at the van. "Righteous wheels you've got there, bro."

Hickok didn't respond.

"You wouldn't want to part with it, would you?"

A grin twisted the gunfighter's lips. "Get real, dude," he said, mimicking Dezi.

The scrawny man ignored the taunt. "What would you take for the van?"

"It's not for sale."

"Then how about a swap. Your wheels look to be in fine shape. We'll swap you any two of ours for yours."

"It's not for trade."

Dezi's eyes narrowed. "We're always in the market for newer, hotter wheels. We want yours."

"No way."

"You'd better think again," Dezi warned, and motioned to the three vehicles to his rear. "You're outnumbered, dude. If you don't agree to our terms, we'll take the van."

Hickok sighed. "Never count your chickens until they're hatched."

"You don't think we can take it?" Dezi asked arrogantly. "There are eleven of us. How many buddies do you have in the van?" He paused and snorted. "Hell, man. We've got hand grenades. If you don't swap us, we'll blow your wheels apart.

Hot wheels like that either belong to us or they don't belong to anyone. Get me?''

Hickok resisted an urge to plug the varmint in the head. The road warriors didn't know about the SEAL's capabilities; they figured they had the upper hand. He was of a mind to teach them the error of their ways. ''I don't want our van damaged.''

''There's the spirit,'' Dezi declared. ''Why not make this easy on all of us? Agree to a trade and you can ride away unharmed.''

''I'll have to talk to my pards.''

''Be my guest,'' Dezi said graciously. ''I'll wait right here.''

Hickok wheeled and strode to the transport. He opened the door, nodded at Dezi, and climbed in.

''What's up?'' Geronimo asked.

''Those gents want to trade two of their buggies for the SEAL,'' Hickok revealed. He laid the Henry on the console and shifted into gear.

''Did you tell them to get stuffed?'' Geronimo queried.

''I told them I'd talk to you.''

''You what?'' Geronimo responded in disbelief.

''They've got grenades.''

''Oh,'' Geronimo said, and began rolling down his window.

Hickok gestured at Dezi. ''The pipsqueak, there, thinks we have a hot set of wheels.'' He chuckled. ''I reckon I'll show him just how hot.''

''What's going on?'' Marcus asked, perplexed by the conversation.

''Use my Henry,'' Hickok instructed him. He quickly rolled down his window.

''I don't get it,'' Marcus said. He grabbed the rifle and leaned between the bucket seats. ''Are we taking these guys on?''

''Yep!''

''All right!''

''Remind me when we get back to the Home to have a long talk with you about your lack of enthusiasm,'' Hickok said, and looked at Geronimo. ''Are you ready, pard?''

''I was born ready.''

''Good grief. Whatever Marcus has is contagious,'' Hickok

cracked. He poked his head out of the window. "Do you promise you'll let us skedaddle unharmed?" he shouted.

"I promise," Dezi responded, grinning maliciously. "Drive the van over here, but do it slowly."

"Here we come," Hickok said, and pressed lightly on the accelerator.

"Why are you playing along with that idiot?" Marcus inquired.

"Heavy Death Rules," Hickok replied.

"Huh?"

The gunman glanced at Geronimo. "What's the range on the flamethrower again?"

"The Operations Manual claimed twenty feet."

"Let's put it to the test," Hickok said. He drove a few yards and braked. "This should be about right."

"What the hell are you doing?" Dezi yelled, waving them on. "Drive the van to me."

The machine gunners in the pickup and the occupants of the two cars all pointed their weapons at the transport.

Hickok grinned and stuck his head out again. "Guess what! I've changed my mind. I don't want to trade."

Dezi took a step forward and raised the Winchester. "Don't mess with us, bastard! We'll blow you to pieces if you screw around. Ask anybody. We're mean mothers!" he declared proudly.

"No, you're rump roast," Hickok corrected him, and reached to his right to flick the toggle activating the flamethrower. He heard a hissing noise, and an instant later a sheet of red and orange flame erupted from the front of the SEAL, engulfing Dezi entirely.

The Warriors listened to the raspy screams as the scrawny man was incinerated on the spot.

Hickok let up on the toggle and tromped on the accelerator, and the transport responded immediately, racing at the three vehicles blocking the highway. He swerved to the left, intending to drive on the strip of weeds between the road and the forest, and gave Geronimo a clear field of fire.

Stunned by the grisly demise of their leader, the Cruisers were sluggish in bringing their weapons to bear.

Geronimo rested the barrel of the FNC on the window, waited until the SEAL was within three yards of the first car, and squeezed the trigger. The burst riddled the windshield and the passenger side, the rounds stitching the man in the front seat and slamming him onto his back.

A beefy Cruiser in the back seat was in the act of pulling the pin on a hand grenade.

"Grenade!" Geronimo bellowed, and sent a withering spray of lead into the back seat, perforating the Cruiser's chest and neck. The man dropped, still holding the grenade. "Move!"

Hickok kept the pedal to the floor. The SEAL sped past the pickup and the second car, and he angled onto Highway Three and shot eastward. He looked in the rear view mirror just as the grenade detonated, and he saw the lead car explode, saw the ball of fire and the shower of metal pieces intermixed with body parts. "One down," he said under his breath, hoping the explosion also took care of the other two vehicles.

"Here they come!" Marcus exclaimed.

The brown pickup and the second car, a battered Ford, roared out of the dust in pursuit of the SEAL.

"Marcus, show them what will happen if they get too close," Hickok directed.

Marcus squeezed over the gunfighter's left shoulder and eased his head and arms out the window. The wind tore at his face and khaki shirt. He elevated the 44-40, snuggled the stock against his right shoulder, and tried to get a bead on the Ford, which was closing rapidly. The bouncing of the SEAL made the barrel dance wildly no matter how hard he attempted to hold it steady.

"What are you doing?" Hickok shouted. "Admiring the scenery?"

Exasperated, Marcus fired, not really expecting to hit anything, the rifle bucking against his shoulder. To his astonishment he saw the Ford abruptly career from the road and barrel at the trees on the north side.

"Not bad," Hickok complimented him.

But the gunman spoke too soon. The Ford corrected its course and resumed the chase, speeding recklessly in an effort to make up the ground lost.

The pickup was still coming on strong. The three machine gunners were using the top of the cab for support, their weapons aimed at the rear of the transport, holding their fire until they narrowed the range.

Marcus aimed at the pickup and squeezed off a shot.

Nothing happened.

"Get in here," Hickok ordered.

Reluctantly, Marcus complied. He sank on his seat and frowned. "I couldn't nail them."

"No foolin'?" Hickok responded.

"The pickup is gaining," Geronimo announced.

The gunfighter glanced over his right shoulder at the onrushing vehicle. "Marcus, forget the Henry. We'll try one of your pigstickers."

"One of my machetes against a pickup truck?"

"Do you have any brighter ideas?" Hickok asked.

"No," Marcus admitted, "but how—"

"Get ready!" Hickok barked, his eyes glued to the rear view mirror. He estimated the pickup to be slightly less than 15 yards from the SEAL. Both vehicles were doing in excess of 70 miles per hour.

Marcus slid his right machete from its sheath and leaned over the gunman.

"Don't show yourself yet," Hickok admonished. "Wait until I give the word."

"My machete won't make a dent in the truck," Marcus noted.

"Go for one of the cow chips in the bed," Hickok directed, watching the pickup. The machine gunners, evidently confident a sustained fusillade at close proximity would disable the transport, fired in unison. The rounds smacked into the impervious green shell and zinged off. They emptied their magazines and went to replace the spent clips.

Which was exactly what the gunman wanted.

Hickok swerved slightly to the right, tromped on the brake, and yelled, ''Now!''

Marcus needed no encouragement. He understood the part he was to play. The instant the SEAL started to slow, he bent his torso out the window, the machete clenched in both hands, and faced the hurtling pickup.

The gunfighter's strategy worked flawlessly.

Taken unaware by the van's unexpected braking, the driver of the pickup couldn't stop in time. The truck came abreast of the transport in the twinkling of an eye, passing within two feet of the SEAL. With their machine guns empty, the three Cruisers on the bed could do no more than gape in stupefaction as they passed the van.

Marcus tucked his back against the SEAL and sucked in his gut. He ignored the speeding truck, ignored the fact he would be crushed if either vehicle deviated from its course by even a few inches, and focused on the nearest man in the pickup bed.

The Cruiser endeavored to throw himself out of harm's way.

Marcus slashed the machete in a wide arc, the blade glistening in the sunlight, the razor edge connecting, biting deep into the machine gunner's neck. The combined force of Marcus's swing, the reverse thrust of the braking SEAL, and the momentum of the racing pickup enabled Marcus to execute a feat he'd never before performed. He decapitated the Cruiser.

Trailed by a geyser of gushing blood, the machine gunner's head sailed high into the air, then fell end over end to the asphalt and bounced down the center of the highway. The headless body swayed for several seconds, then toppled backwards into the bed, its arms outstretched. The driver of the truck finally applied the brakes, causing the remaining machine gunners to lose their balance and fall on top of the headless corpse.

''Piece of cake!'' Hickok stated. He angled the SEAL in behind the pickup and activated the 50-caliber machine guns mounted under the headlights.

The result was a slaughter. The slugs punched through the tailgate and the rear of the cab, drilling into the two Cruisers in the bed as they attempted to scramble to their feet and slaying the driver before he could take evasive action.

Hickok accelerated again, bypassing the pickup on the right. He saw the driver of the truck slumped over the steering wheel, and he stared at the van's side mirror as the SEAL sped to the east. The pickup slowed to a crawl, then slanted to the north and left the road. It coasted to a stop a yard shy of the tree line.

"The Ford is still on our tail," Geronimo declared.

Hickok shifted his attention to the rearview mirror. "I see it," he said. The armored car was 40 yards behind the transport and reducing the distance swiftly.

"These guys don't give up easily," Marcus commented.

"Just what we needed," Hickok muttered. "Persistent psychos."

"Do you have any more tricks up your sleeve?" Marcus asked.

"Just the obvious," the gunman said.

"What's that?"

"You'll see in a bit, as soon as I find what I need," Hickok said. He spotted an abandoned, dilapidated house 200 feet ahead, on the south side of the road. "And this could be it. Geronimo, get ready to grab the wheel."

"Why?"

Hickok noted the overgrown weeds surrounding the house. He scrutinized the front yard, a stretch of tangled brush, and distinguished the curved contours of an asphalt driveway. "I'm bailin' out."

"You're crazy," Marcus interjected.

"We can't afford any more blasted delays," Hickok stated. "I want to end this nonsense and head for Boston."

Thirty yards separated the SEAL from the Ford.

Hickok gripped the wheel tightly, gauging the distance of the driveway. He wondered if the Cruisers in the Ford possessed hand grenades. A single accurate toss and the SEAL would be totaled. He would have to dispose of the Cruisers before they could throw, requiring split-second timing.

"I hope you know what you're doing," Geronimo said, then added with a smirk, "for once."

"Are you kiddin'? Every move I make is planned," Hickok fibbed.

"It's getting deep in here," Geronimo remarked, gazing at the Ford.

"Then I'd best leave before my moccasins get all smelly," Hickok joked. He braced for the turn and shouted, "Hang on!" Then he arrowed the transport toward the driveway and wrenched on the steering wheel at the very last instant. The SEAL took the corner on two wheels and almost flipped over. Hickok slid against the door. A moment later the transport settled on all four tires. He buried the brake pedal and the van lurched to a precipitate stop. "Take over," he yelled, and vaulted from the SEAL, leaving the gearshift in Drive. Every second was crucial. He hit the ground running and dashed toward the highway, drawing the Colts as he ran.

The Cruiser driving the Ford was on the ball. Although the gunman's maneuver caught the man by surprise, the driver only overshot the driveway by a few yards. A burly man carrying a grenade leaped from the armored car the second it halted.

Hickok reached the end of the driveway and swiveled toward the Ford, thumbing back the hammers, and he fired both revolvers as the burly man went to pull the pin on the grenade. The slugs slammed the Cruiser into the armored car and the man slumped to the road. Without slowing, Hickok sprinted to the Ford and moved along the driver's side.

A Cruiser armed with a rifle stuck the barrel out the open rear window and snapped off a shot.

Hickok was already somewhere else. He dove for the ground a hair's breadth before the rifle boomed, and he landed hard on his elbows and knees and rolled onto his back, aiming the Pythons straight up at the grimy face framed in the car window. The Colts cracked and the man was flung from view.

The driver, apparently deciding that his life was more important then revenge, floored the Ford.

The gunfighter rose, tracking the armored car, his arms extended, wanting to be sure. He could see the driver's window, but he didn't have a clear shot. If the man would look back once, just once, he could put an end to the Cruisers.

The man did. Grinning broadly, as if he was gloating, confident he had escaped, the driver glanced over his left shoulder at the Warrior.

A fatal mistake.

The Pythons discharged. Hickok felt the revolvers buck and saw the driver's head snap around. The Ford cut to the right, doing over 50, crossed the edge of the highway, and smashed into the base of a towering pine tree with a tremendous crash. "Got you," Hickok said softly.

Marcus dashed to the gunman's side. "I thought you might need some help." He gazed at the wrecked Ford. "I should have known better."

Hickok twirled the Pythons into their holsters. "Let's reload the rocket-launcher and the 50-calibers and get the heck out of here."

"How long will it take us to reach Boston?" Marcus asked idly.

"At the rate we're going, we'll be lucky if we reach Boston before Christmas," Hickok snapped. "We have to pick up the pace. I have a bad feeling that Blade is in a heap of trouble."

Chapter Thirteen

"Doctor Milton? Nurse Krittenbauer?" the guard repeated. "Are you all right? I heard a noise."

Berwin was livid. He glared at Milton and whispered instructions. "Tell him everything is fine. Tell him you dropped a book or something. If you try to shout, to alert him in any way, I'll break your neck as if it was a twig. Do you understand?"

The physician, his eyes wide, nodded.

"Your life depends on what you do next," Berwin warned, and relaxed his hold on the man's neck.

Milton licked his lips, then coughed. "We're busy, Private Nelson. We don't want to be disturbed," he called out.

"Sorry, sir," Nelson replied. "I thought I heard a loud noise."

"I accidentally bumped a pile of books onto the floor," Milton declared. "If we need you, we'll let you know."

"Yes, sir," Nelson said. "Sorry. I won't bother you again."

Berwin listened intently, allowing the guard time to return to his post near the elevator. "Okay, Doctor. Sit in this chair," he commanded, and pointed at the chair Krittenbauer had used.

Milton promptly obeyed, rubbing his sore neck, clearly nervous. "I'll do whatever you want." He glanced at the KGB agent, at the blood dribbling from her mouth. "Just don't hurt me."

"You're a brave man, Doctor," Blade said sarcastically.

"I'm not accustomed to violence."

"You're in the military."

"Yes, but I'm a scientist involved in medical research, not a fighter," Milton said. His eyes narrowed and he regarded the giant carefully. "Wait a minute. How did you know I'm in the military?"

"You'd be surprised at what I know," Berwin replied.

Milton sighed and folded his hands in his lap. "I dreaded this happening."

"Dreaded what?" Berwin asked, sitting on the edge of the desk.

"Your natural personality asserting itself," Milton said. "Your aggressive tendencies have negated the effect of the drug."

"Tell me about the Memroxin."

Milton frowned. "Memroxin is an experimental drug we've developed to extract information from recalcitrant subjects. You were administered a dose shortly after your capture."

"My capture?"

"Yes. The HGP Unit captured you near the Home. If it's any consolation, I heard that you resisted admirably," Milton said. "They were flown to Minnesota by helicopter specifically for the purpose of taking you prisoner. The general was quite adamant about capturing you. He didn't want anyone else."

Berwin's forehead creased as he sorted the new information. If he'd been captured in Minnesota, then he must *be* from Minnesota, from the Home the scientist had mentioned. None of the revelations jarred his memory. He realized he must proceed cautiously. If Milton knew how little he truly knew, the colonel might lie to keep him in the dark. "It sounds as if the general doesn't like me," he commented.

Milton snorted. "Like you? General Malenkov despises you

and the rest of the Family. But he especially hates you because of the many times you have thwarted his plans. Oh. And there is one other he hates. The Warrior named Hickok.''

The name provoked a recognition response in Berwin's mind. He recalled the blond man in buckskins he'd seen in his dream, and he perceived the two were one and the same. Hickok. He felt the man was a close friend, although he couldn't remember any experiences they had shared.

"There is a rumor making the rounds, and I don't know how true it is, that General Malenkov became furious after you destroyed Lenin's Needle in Cincinnati. He vowed to take revenge on you and the Family, at all costs.''

Lenin's Needle? The title was unfamiliar to Berwin.

"General Malenkov personally conceived of the intricate plan to eradicate your Family once and for all,'' Milton went on. "He sent the HGP Unit to capture you, and you were transported to Boston and placed in the HGP ward under my care.''

"Why Boston? Why you?''

"I was placed in charge of your treatment because I was instrumental in creating the Memroxin. No one knows the capabilities of the drug better than I do.''

"What are its capabilities?''

"Memroxin inhibits the ability to remember past events. You might say its a form of induced amnesia. Twelve hours after Memroxin is injected, the subject can't remember a thing. Bewilderment and disorientation are quite common.''

"How many doses was I given?''

"One. One dose is all that's required. Our experiments demonstrated that additional amounts of Memroxin don't enhance its effectiveness one iota.''

"How long does the amnesia last?''

Milton had relaxed as they conversed. He gestured absently, as if he was lecturing an intern. "The duration varies. For maximum effectiveness the subject must be kept in a controlled environment where all external stimulation is eliminated. You see, the potency of the Memroxin is reduced when the subject is subjected to strong emotional affirmation of the previous identity.''

"In other words, if someone the subject knew and loved were to walk into the subject's room, the Memroxin would lose its hold?''

"It could happen. Even favorite possessions can trigger recall.''

Berwin pondered for a moment. "I don't get it. How can the Memroxin be used to extract information if it makes the subject forget everything?''

"There's the beauty of the drug,'' Milton stated proudly. "The subject gradually begins to recall events, people, and places from the past, but the memories are vague at first. They take the form of dreams or random associations, and they're of no unusual significance to the subject.'' He paused. "That's where I come in. If properly manipulated, the subject will reveal a host of important information he or she ordinarily wouldn't divulge. To the subjects, there is no connection between their dreams and their past.''

"That's why you were so interested in my dreams.''

"Exactly.''

"And all the lies you told me?''

"They were intended to allay any suspicions you might have entertained. We fabricated the report of your demolition accident to explain your presence in the hospital—''

"But what about my scar?'' Berwin interrupted, running his finger along the indentation.

Milton smiled. "It's fake. We shaved some of your hair off, and a professional makeup artist applied the phony scar. If you use your thumbnail, you can peel the scar right off.''

Berwin jabbed his right thumbnail into the skin at the nape of his neck, just below where the scar began. In seconds he succeeded in peeling the tip off, and a sharp tug removed the remainder. He dangled the strip of flesh-colored adhesive material in his hand, reflecting on the brilliance of the deception.

"Your so-called family also figured in our scheme. We wanted you to feel at ease, to avoid arousing your Warrior nature. We thought you would adjust more readily if you believed you had the support of a loving family,'' Milton disclosed.

''And the lie about the United States winning World War Three was to convince me the Russians couldn't possibly be a threat, just in case some memory of the war surfaced?''

Milton nodded. ''And to convince you that you were among fellow citizens in a country to which you were devoted. We hoped to eliminate any suggestion of a potentially disturbing memory of a hostile nature. Our enemies can arouse strong emotions too.''

''And strong emotions interfere with the Memroxin.''

''What triggered your memory?'' Milton inquired. ''Was it something the damn janitor said?''

''I'll ask the questions,'' Berwin rejoined stiffly.

''Oh. Sorry.''

''Why did you go to so much trouble to get the information you wanted out of me? Why not use truth serum or simple torture?''

''Because General Malenkov gave explicit instructions that you weren't to be harmed under any circumstances. So torture, obviously, was out. Truth serum, as you call it, is not all it's cracked up to be. It's unreliable. The subject can resist, even lie. And there are sometimes adverse side effects. Memroxin, on the other hand, is harmless, and eventually the subject regains a fully restored memory.''

Berwin stared at the scientist. ''Why does General Malenkov want me in one piece?''

''Because of the part you're to play in the HGP Project,'' Milton answered.

''What's that?''

''The HGP Project is the second reason you were brought to Boston. HGP research is based in Boston, and this hospital, specifically this ward, is exclusively devoted to the Project.''

''Explain.''

''I wouldn't know where to begin.''

''Try the beginning,'' Berwin suggested.

''Very well. Prior to the war, American scientists in this very city were earnestly engaged in the Human Genome Project, or HGP. Do you know what a human genome is?"

"No."

"The human genome refers to the complete set of genetic instructions for making a human being. Billions of dollars were spent by American scientists in the decade preceding the war as they attempted to map and sequence every human gene. They made commendable progress, despite the magnitude of the task. There are approximately one hundred thousand genes in the human body, and there are about three billion chemical components of genetic material. The goal is to identify every one."

"Why?"

"Think of the implications. Eventually we'll be able to take a fragment of tissue from an embryo and screen it for every known disease based on its genetic constitution. There are around four thousand heritable diseases in the world, and we intend to track down the genetic base of each. Through selective breeding we can ultimately eliminate those diseases," Milton boasted.

Berwin straightened when he heard the phrase "selective breeding." "Eliminate the diseases? How?"

"By terminating every embryo carrying a genetic defect."

"Mass abortions?"

Milton nodded and grinned. "Why do you look so shocked? Mass abortions were commonplace in America before the war. Over two million babies were aborted every year. We are simply continuing the work the Americans started."

"How do I fit into the picture?"

"I assume you know about our Impregnation Program?"

Berwin frowned. "Yeah, I know about it," he said distastefully.

"Well, twenty-five years ago we combined certain aspects of the Impregnation Program with the Human Genome Project. The result was an elite squad of perfect soldiers, our HGP Unit."

"I don't follow you."

"Imagine, if you will, a squad of highly trained commandos, every one of which is a perfect physical specimen," Milton said. "We started screening embryos two and a half decades ago, looking for those without genetic blemish. The task hasn't been an easy one. With so many thousands of heritable diseases, finding embryos totally free from such traits is akin to looking for the proverbial needle in a haystack." He paused. "But we have been moderately successful. There are currently eighteen soldiers in the HGP Unit. Supersoldiers would be a more accurate description, physically superb in every respect. Each one is the equal of four ordinary soldiers. Their strength, their endurance, their mental alacrity are all far above normal."

"I still don't see where I fit in," Blade observed.

"We've discovered that we increase our chances of obtaining flawless embryos if the paternal factors contributing to the production of the embryos meet certain criteria. For instance, impregnating a healthy, intelligent woman with the sperm from a man who is endowed with an above-average intellect and a healthy body greatly increases the odds of producing a perfect embryo. Impregnating a slovenly cow with the sperm from an imbecile defeats our purposes," Milton stated, and smirked at his last comment.

Berwin slowly stood, his fists clenched at his sides. "You were planning to use me in your program? You were going to use my sperm to breed your supersoldiers?"

"Yes," Milton confirmed. "General Malenkov came up with the idea. First he wanted us to extract all the information we could pertaining to the layout of the Home for the HGP Unit to use when they conduct their raid. Then the general wanted us to extract semen, which we would use to impregnate selected females. We ran two complete series of tests on you, and our tests have proven you to be an ideal candidate for the HGP Project. Which wasn't very surprising. You're seven feet tall and endowed with a herculean physique. On top of that, your IQ is in the genius range."

"Says who?"

"Don't be modest. You know you're superior to ninety-nine

percent of humanity."

"I know nothing of the sort. I'm no better or worse than most people. I'm just ordinary."

Milton laughed. "Sure you are! Who's deluding whom?"

Berwin folded his arms and studied the scientist, thinking of additional questions he needed to ask. "When is the HGP Unit slated to conduct the raid?"

"The general is waiting for the data I was to extract from you. He thought it highly appropriate that information you supplied would be employed to destroy the Family."

"Where is the HGP Unit based?"

Milton did a double take. "Why do you want to know?"

"Answer me," Berwin said, his tone low and grating.

"They're billeted at Gorbachev Air Force Base, northwest of the city. They're kept on alert status twenty-four hours a day so they can depart whenever the need arises. A fleet of helicopters is always at their disposal," Milton said. "They utilized one of their specially modified choppers when they captured you, a helicopter with an extended flight range. I was told they refueled in Illinois, then flew close to the Home. One of the women pretended to be in distress and you responded to her cries for help."

"There are female supersoldiers?"

"Certainly. Would you accuse us of genetic discrimination?"

"No. I could accuse you of being immoral genetic fascists, but that's beside the point. What happened after the woman yelled for help?"

"You were suckered into the forest and shot with a tranquilizer dart. Actually, you were shot with three tranquilizer darts. They misjudged the proper dose required to render you unconscious, and you proved difficult to subdue. Two of the HGP Unit sustained broken limbs," Milton divulged. "After you were down, they carted you to the helicopter. You were flown directly here, except for a few refueling stops."

"Who administered the Memroxin to me?"

"I injected it."

Berwin leaned down until his nose was an inch from the

scientist's. "I should do the world a favor and kill you right here and now."

Milton swallowed hard and squirmed in the chair. "I don't want to die."

"Do you think I care what you want? How many American women have you impregnated against their will? How many people have suffered as guinea pigs in your damnable experiments?"

"I'm not personally involvled with the impregnations," Milton said defensively. He detected a steely cast to the Warrior's gray eyes, and he expected those brawny hands to clamp on his neck again. Fearful for his life, well aware of the Warrior's reputation, he frantically sought a diversionary tactic, anything to take the giant's mind off of his part in the HGP Project. He blurted out the first thing that came into his head. "Would you like your own clothes back?"

"Do you have them?"

"In there," Milton said, and nodded at the closet.

Berwin walked over. "Which ones?" he asked, scrutinizing the uniforms and other clothing, none of which he recognized.

"The black leather vest and the fatigue pants hanging on the far right side are yours," Milton revealed. "So are the combat boots on the floor in the right corner."

Berwin moved a white smock aside and found the vest and pants. For a second he thought he recalled wearing the vest before, but the second passed and the blank slate mocked him again. He took both garments and placed them on the oaken desk, then retrieved the combat boots. Eager to remove the uncomfortable clothing he had on, he glanced at the scientist. "Bend over."

"What?"

"I don't want you to try to escape while I'm changing," Berwin explained. "Bend over, wrap your arms around your legs, and close your eyes. If you so much as twitch before I give the word, I'll split your skull open."

"I won't give you any trouble," Milton promised as he bent down. "I'll help you in any way I can. Just don't kill me.

Please.''

"Be quiet," Berwin directed. He hurriedly stripped off the flannel shirt, jeans, and brown boots, discarding them on the floor, and donned the fatigue pants, the black leather vest, and finally the combat boots, sitting on the desk as he tied the laces. "Are there any weapons in here?"

Despite the injuction to keep his eyes closed, Milton looked up, his features reflecting alarm. "Weapons?"

"Yeah. You know. Guns. Grenades. Tanks. Atomic bombs. Anything?"

"This is my office. I'm not a soldier," Milton said.

Berwin stood, his suspicions aroused by the scientist's evasive behavior. "So there aren't any weapons in here?"

"No," Milton asserted, and glanced at the desk.

"I hope you're telling me the truth," Berwin stated, stepping around to the opposite side. There were six small drawers, three on each side.

"The guard has a gun," Milton mentioned hastily.

"I've been meaning to ask you about the guard," Berwin remarked. "Why is he wearing a blue uniform from a place called Acme Security instead of a Russian uniform?"

Milton gripped the arms of his chair tightly, watching the giant's every move. "We issued civilian security guard uniforms to every soldier assigned to corridor duty in case you were to stumble onto them."

"Is that a fact?" Berwin responded. He opened the top drawer on the left and found only papers.

"Why don't you disarm the guard?" Milton queried nervously.

Berwin opened the second drawer on the left, which was crammed with pens, papers, and two paperback books: a dictionary and a volume of biological terminology.

"I don't keep weapons in my desk," Milton said, and laughed, a fake, brittle sound betraying his rising anxiety.

Why was the man so upset? Berwin asked himself. He inspected the final drawer on the left and discovered several pill bottles, a packet of tongue depressors, and a box of gauze.

"You wouldn't lie to me, would you, Doctor?"

"Of course not," Milton stated.

Berwin reached for the top drawer on the right.

"I'll even lure the guard in here for you," Milton proposed. "How about that?"

"Your kindness overwhelms me," Berwin quipped, and yanked the drawer open.

Milton gasped.

There were two of them, a matched set, lying on top of a stack of medical forms, each still in a leather sheath, lying flat, side by side.

Bowie knives.

A tingle rippled along Berwin's spine, as if he'd received an electric shock. "My name isn't Berwin, is it, Doctor?" he asked.

"No," Milton answered hoarsely.

"What is my real name?" the giant inquired. He grasped the Bowies, one in each hand, and raised them into the light. The moment he did, a veritable explosion of memories filled his mind. In the space of a heartbeat the blank slate was gone. In its place, flooding his consciousness with the irresistible force of a whirlpool, dazzling him with intensity and vividness, was his past.

He remembered!

Chapter Fourteen

The Warrior sensed another presence.

He sat in the lotus position on a knoll in the pristine eastern section of the Home, the portion preserved in its natural state, and meditated on the path of the perfected swordmaster. His brown eyes were closed, his hands on his knees. In his lap was his prized katana. His shirt, pants, and shoes, sewn together by the Family Weavers and patterned after martial arts uniforms he'd seen in books in the Family Library, were black.

Yes, he decided after several seconds, keeping his eyes closed so as not to alert whoever—or whatever—was watching him, there definitely was another presence nearby. But how could it be? Few were the creatures that could get close to him undetected. As a perfected swordsman, he had diligently sharpened his physical senses to a superlative degree. In addition, his sixth sense, the instinctive faculty every Warrior possessed to a greater or lesser degree, invariably flared if danger threatened.

What could possibly elude detection?

Ever so slowly the Warrior inched his right hand to the hilt of his katana.

"Whoa, there, chuckles! Don't do anything I'll regret!"

The diminutive Warrior opened his eyes and smiled at the hybrid standing six feet away. "To what do I owe this honor, Lynx?"

The cat-man advanced and sat down in front of the swordsman. "Sorry to interrupt your thinkin', but I wanted to talk to you, Rikki."

Rikki-Tikki-Tavi released the katana and eyed the mutation speculatively. "Obviously."

Lynx gazed up at the sky, then at the east wall of the Home visible through the trees rimming the knoll. "Nice spot. Do you come here often?"

"On a dialy basis when feasible," Rikki said. "This is my favorite spot for communing with the Spirit."

Lynx coughed. "Yeah, well, I never did put much stock in all that spirit jazz. I was created in a test tube. What do I do? Worship glass?"

Rikki grinned. "Each of us must find our own path."

"Have you found yours?"

"Yes. I'm a Warrior."

"So am I. Which is what I'd like to talk about. I've got a gripe."

"Then you should wait until Blade returns and lodge your complaint with him," Rikki advised.

"*If* he returns, I will," Lynx said. "But before I do, I want to get you on my side."

"I thought we're all on the same side."

"Don't go gettin' philosophical with me. I looked you up because I figured you could help us with our problem."

"Us?"

"Gremlin, Ferret, and me."

"Do they share your complaint?" Rikki asked.

"You bet," Lynx assured him. "They're with me one hundred percent."

"Where are they now? I thought the three of you were inseparable," Rikki commented.

"We are. But we, uh, decided that just one of us should talk to you, and here I am."

"What's bothering you?"

Lynx pointed at the katana. "You get to use your toothpick a lot, don't you?"

Rikki placed his right hand on the smooth scabbard. "I practice daily. As a Warrior I can't permit my skills to atrophy. My life, and the lives of those for whom I care, depend on my expertise."

"That wasn't quite what I meant. Sure, you practice a lot, but you also get to use your sword, your skills, in combat. You've been on a lot or runs with Blade and the others."

"What's your point?"

Lynx looked down at the grass and grinned slyly, then stared at the Family's consummate martial artist with a straight face. "My point is that your skills don't atrophy because you have the chance to use them. Practice is fine, but all the practice in the world ain't about to replace the real thing. There's no substitute for actual combat. We're Warriors. We kick butt for a livin'. And if we're not given the chance, we can get sloppy."

"True," Rikki said, and smiled. "I had no idea the spirit of the samurai animates your soul."

"Huh?"

"I had no idea you were so devoted to our craft."

"Yeah, well, I've got all kinds of devotion. Just because I'm covered with fur and have pointy teeth and claws doesn't mean I'm not a person. I have feelings, too, you know."

"I meant no insult," Rikki said.

"None taken, pal. Now will you help us out or not?"

"You still haven't told me how I can be of service," Rikki reminded the cat-man.

"Oh. Well, it's like this. Gremlin, Ferret, and me haven't seen much action lately. Hell, I haven't wasted any chumps since Houston. We're overdue," Lynx elaborated. "We need to get out in the field to keep ourselves in fighting trim."

Rikki-Tikki-Tavi reflected for a moment. As a man who had spent most of his life honing his skills at dispensing death, he could relate to Lynx's complaint. For a Warrior inactivity was the bane of existence. Inactivity bred complacency, complacency bred boredom, and boredom bred diffidence. Such a state of affairs could well prove fatal to those who lived by the keenness of their wits and the quickness of their sinews. "You have a valid point. How may I help?"

"You can talk to Blade for us."

"In what respect?"

"Gremlin, Ferret, and me want to go on the next run," Lynx stated.

Rikki pursed his lips, then replied, "I don't know if I can be of any aid."

"Why not?"

"Blade decides who will go on the runs. He has the last, the *only* word on the matter. A few times he's drawn straws to determine who would go on particularly dangerous missions. I doubt whether I can convince him to take you," Rikki said.

"I'm not askin' you to convince Blade. All I want you to do is put in a good word for us," Lynx clarified.

"No problem."

Lynx leaned forward excitedly. "All you have to do is point out that a few of the Warriors haven't been on runs yet. Gremlin, Ferret, and me ain't the only ones. It's only fair that we all should go, isn't it?"

"I see no reason why you shouldn't," Rikki said.

"Good. If I can ever do a favor for you, all you have to do is ask."

"That won't be necessary."

"I pay my debts," Lynx declared, then glanced around to ensure they were alone. "There is one more thing you could do, if you don't mind."

Rikki's eyes narrowed. "What?"

"When you bring up the subject to Blade, don't tell him I asked you to do it."

"Why not?"

Lynx gestured, bending his arms and holding his hands palms outward. "You know how the Big Dummy is. He's liable to accuse me of stickin' my big nose in where it doesn't belong."

"Blade is a fair man. He'd understand your feelings."

"Yeah. Maybe. But why rock the boat? Just casually mention your opinion that the Warriors who haven't been on runs should get to go and leave it at that."

"As you wish."

"Terrific!" Lynx said happily. He took hold of Rikki's right hand and pumped vigorously. "We can never thank you enough. Gremlin, Ferret, and me will pay you back, somehow."

"There's no need," Rikki responded.

"Hey, what are buddies for?" Lynx asked, and rose. "I'll let you go back to your thinkin'." He started to the west and gave a little wave of his left hand. "Thanks again."

"Be seeing you."

Lynx walked down the knoll and entered the woods below. The intant he was out of the martial artist's sight, he rubbed his hands together and snickered in triumph. His plan was working like a charm! Gremlin and Ferret were going to go on a mission with him whether they liked the idea or not. He intended to insure Blade got the message. Let's see, he mentally noted. So far he had talked to Yama, Bertha, and Sundance. Who should he make his pitch to next? He came to a clearing and glanced to the north, and far off he saw a powerfully built Warrior attired in a camouflage outfit walking along the northern rampart. The Warrior's brown hair fell to the small of his broad back.

Lynx chuckled.

Ahhhhhh, yes. Samson.

Chapter Fifteen

He remembered!

He remembered his lovely wife, Jenny, and his energetic son, Gabe, and he was momentarily saddened by the thought of them being so many miles away. He remembered the joyous years of his childhood at the Home, and the many hours he spent playing with his constant companions, Hickok and Geronimo. He remembered the sorrow he'd experienced when his father had been slain by a mutation, and the abiding friendship he'd developed with his mentor, the Family Leader, Plato. He remembered the many missions he had been on in his capacity as the head Warrior, and especially the times he had fought the Russians. But most important of all, he remembered and concentrated on the Naming ceremony held on his sixteenth birthday.

Kurt Carpenter had initiated the Naming ceremony. The Founder instituted the practice of formally christening every Family member at the age of 16 as a means of guaranteeing his followers and their descendents would never lose sight of their historical antecedents. Carpenter had worried that subsequent generations might lose sight of the reasons for the Family's existence. He was afraid they would forget their roots, that they would shun any reference to World War Three and prior eras and never learn the valuable lessons history could teach them. In an effort to spark an interest in history, in the causes and circumstances responsible for the decline of civilization, Carpenter prompted his followers to encourage their children to scour the history books and select the name of any historical figure they liked as their very own. In the decades since the war the practice had been expanded so that the 16-year-olds could pick a name from any source they desired. Family members weren't forced to choose a new name, but most did. A few kept the names bestowed on them by their parents. Even fewer opted for renaming themselves with an original name they preferred.

Carpenter had also advocated abolishing surnames. In his estimation last names created a false civility and fabricated respect. Every Family member was entitled to one name only. Thus 16-year-old Nathan, a virtuoso with revolvers and an ardent admirer of the Old West, chose the name of the man he considered to be the greatest gunman of all time, a gent called Hickok. Sixteen-year-old Lone Elk selected the name of the historical figure he esteemed the highest, Geronimo. And a youth known as Michael picked an entirely new name based on the affinity for edged weapons, particularly his fondness for Bowie knives, and called himself . . . Blade.

"My name is Blade," the giant said softly, more to himself than the scientist, and a peculiar constriction formed in his throat. "My name is *Blade.*"

"Now you know," Milton remarked nervously. "I suspected those knives might trigger your memory, so I kept them handy."

Blade placed the Bowies on the desk and stripped off his belt. "Where's Malenkov?"

Milton tensed and blinked a few times. "What?"

"You heard me," Blade said. He threaded the belt through the loops on his fatigue pants, aligning a sheath on each hip, and then fastened the buckle.

"Why . . . why do you want to know?" Milton stammered.

The Warrior rested his hands on the Bowie hilts and walked around the desk to stand next to the chair. "Where is General Malenkov?" he demanded coldly.

"Washington! He's in Washington, D.C."

Blade leaned down, his eyes on a level with Milton's. "Why don't I believe you?"

"I'm telling the truth! You must know that he's prominent in the North American Central Committee. He's responsible for administering the occupation forces in America."

"Do tell."

"Surely you know the general operates out of Washington? You were there once and escaped from his clutches."

Blade shook his head. "A friend of mine named Hickok was the one who got away from the general." He paused meaningfully. "I'll take your word that Malenkov isn't in Boston."

Milton exhaled loudly. "Thank you."

"And now I have to escape from Russian territory," Blade said slowly. "But what do I do with you first?"

"Leave me here. Bind me and stick a gag in my mouth. Stuff me in the closet. Do anything you want. Just don't harm me," Milton pleaded.

The giant frowned and straightened.

"I won't try to get loose. I promise," Milton babbled on. "I'll wait for them to find me, and I won't divulge which way you've gone."

"You won't *know* which way I've gone," Blade said, his tone tinged with contempt.

"I'll throw them off the track if you want," Milton proposed. "I'll lie to them, tell them you're going south or west or north or whatever you want. I'll make them—"

Blade held up his right hand for silence, cutting the man off. "Enough."

"Please," Milton begged, and tears welled in the corners of his eyes. "Don't kill me."

"How many innocent lives have you taken, Doctor?"

"I told you. I'm a scientist, not a soldier."

Blade slanted his body so the doctor couldn't see his left side. "You're evading the question. How many people have you killed while conducting your medical research?"

"I never personally killed anyone," Milton said.

Blade tightened his left hand on the left Bowie. "You're still evading the question. How many people have been killed by your research? How many have died to further your quest for knowledge?"

"There are always sacrifices to be made on the altar of progress. Every great stride in science has been attended by the unfortunate deaths of those who contributed their lives to the cause," Milton stated defensively.

"How many did your research kill?"

Milton hesitated, torn between his fear of the giant and his resentment of the Warrior's indictment of his professional ethics. He knew the smart thing to do was lie, but he also knew Blade wouldn't accept his lies and might become angry. "A few unfortunates have perished during the course of scientific programs I've headed."

"How many?"

Milton fidgeted, then shrugged. "I don't recall the exact number."

"Ten?"

"I don't know."

"Fifty?"

"I don't know," Milton snapped, forgetting himself.

"Eighty?"

"Certainly not that many," Milton replied.

"How many died before you perfected the Memroxin? How many totally lost their minds? How many were turned into vegetables?" Blade asked, his left arm poised.

"No more than two dozen, I assure you," Milton said shamelessly. "I always strive to keep the losses at a minimum."

"Damn decent of you," Blade declared, and swept the left Bowie out and around, spinning in a tight arc. He buried the knife in the center of Milton's chest and held on fast.

The scientist stiffened and grunted, then gazed with unblinking eyes at the Warrior's hand and the hilt, stunned. "Why?" he blurted out in a whisper.

"I could cite several reasons, Doctor. Because of what you did to me. Because of what you've done to so many others. Because you're murdering scum who uses the cloak of science to justify his actions. But mainly because you're a coward who inflicts torment on others without feeling the slightest degree of guilt," Blade detailed, and looked into Milton's eyes. He saw the man was fading rapidly. "You were talking about imbeciles earlier, Doctor. Do you remember? I want you to die seeing yourself as you truly are, bastard."

Milton's eyelids fluttered and blood trickled from the right corner of his mouth.

"You're the worst kind of imbecile there is, Doctor," Blade said. "You are a moral imbecile." With that, he wrenched the Bowie free and stood back.

A crimson gusher flowed from Milton's chest, and he gulped for air as if he was a fish out of water. His eyes alighted on the Warrior and his expression became comically quizzical. "I—" he managed to squeak. Then his features hardened into a death mask and he slowly sank forward until his chin rested on his legs.

"Now to get out of here," Blade said to himself. He began to wipe the Bowie clean on Milton's smock.

"You're not going anywhere, you son of a bitch!" snarled a gruff female voice behind him.

Blade started to turn, but a hard object rammed him in the spine and he froze.

"Go ahead!" Nancy Krittenbauer stated. "Give me an excuse to put a hole in you. You deserve to die for what you did to poor Milton and for what you did to me."

The Warrior held the left Bowie close to his waist. Annoyance at his stupidity made him scowl. He'd forgotten all about the KGB agent, and the carelessness could cost him his newfound liberty if he didn't come up with a brainstorm, and quickly.

"Drop your knife," Krittenbauer ordered.

Blade let the Bowie fall.

"Now put your hands on your head."

Again the Warrior complied.

"Walk to the door," Krittenbauer instructed him. "And don't try anything stupid."

Exasperated, Blade took a stride. In the back of his mind he wondered why the KGB agent hadn't made him toss the other Bowie aside. He assumed she wanted to turn him over to the guard and have her injuries tended to promptly. Even so, a professional wouldn't ordinarily permit an enemy to retain a weapon. She probably figured she didn't need to worry because she had him covered.

Or did she?

A thought struck him and he almost halted in surprise. What if Krittenbauer wasn't armed? If she really had a gun, why didn't she pull it when he emerged from the closet? Why had she attempted to alert the guard instead?

What if Krittenbauer was bluffing?

Blade took another step, his mind racing. Once she enlisted the assistance of the guard, escape would become much more difficult. If he was going to make a move, then logic dictated he had to do it before they reached the door. But what if he was wrong? The odds were fifty-fifty that she had a gun. If he miscalculated, he'd wind up with a hole in his back the size of a cantaloupe.

Krittenbauer coughed several times, apparently clearing her throat to shout for the guard.

It was now or never.

The Warrior took one more pace, tensing his arms and legs, then surged into action, taking a step to the left even as he lashed his right fist around. A gun boomed and a bullet tugged at the bottom of his vest, but he ignored the retort and concentrated on completing his turn. He glimpsed Krittenbauer's startled, battered visage, and then his right fist caught her full in the face and catapulted her backwards, her arms swinging wildly.

The KBG agent tripped and collided with the chair on which Milton's corspe sat.

Blade's right hand flashed to the right Bowie. He went to raise

his arm for an overhead toss when he heard the office door
opening. Instantly he swiveled back again and saw the guard,
Nelson, come into the room with his pistol drawn. Blade let
the knife fly, his arm a blur, then spun to confront Krittenbauer.

The KGB agent was just regaining her footing.

In the stress of the moment, Blade couldn't afford to look
at the guard. All he could do was hope his throw had been on
target as he took two swift steps and executed a spinning
roundhouse kick, his right leg snapping out to connect with
Krittenbauer's face. The blow sent her into the chair again.
Dazed, she sagged, a Falcon 45 ACP clutched in her right hand.
Blade moved in and delivered the coup de grace, a swordhand
chop to the left side of her neck.

Something snapped and Krittenbauer's head flopped to the
left.

Blade whirled, ready for the worst, thinking he might have
missed. But he hadn't.

The guard was on his knees, his arms hanging limp, a Beretta
Model 84 lying next to his left hand, his eyes glazing rapidly.
Protruding from the base of his throat, sunk to the hilt, was
the Bowie. His lips moved soundlessly. Blood seeped from his
mouth and gushed from his throat.

Blade hurriedly retrieved his left Bowie and stuck Krittenbauer's Falcon under his belt. He walked to Nelson, added the
Beretta to his collection by aligning the pistol near his left sheath,
then jerked the other Bowie from the guard's neck.

Nelson swayed, the blood spurting from the wound, then fell
onto his face with a muffled thud.

Time to haul butt.

The Warrior took a step toward the door, and only then did
he see the horrified nurse standing in the doorway, her hands
over her mouth. She suddenly darted to the right and he took
off after her. As he came through the door he saw her press a
red button mounted under the counter on a wide shelf, and all
hell broke loose.

The nurse looked at him and screamed in terror.

A raucous din erupted, a cacophony of blaring klaxons,

seeming to emanate from everywhere, filling the air with strident discord.

"Damn!" Blade exclaimed. He bounded to the nurse and slugged her on the chin, knocking her into the counter. She promptly collapsed, out to the world. Well aware that more guards would arrive at any second, Blade placed his hands on the counter and vaulted over it. He glanced at the elevator, chagrined to behold the floor indicator moving from the fourth floor to the third. The car was on its way down to pick up reinforcements!

Now what?

He recalled Milton saying something about stairs, and he sped to the junction and inspected each branch. Off to his right, perhaps 50 feet away, a small sign hung next to a closed door. On a hunch he jogged toward the door. Despite his predicament, despite being hopelessly outnumbered, and despite being half a continent from his loved ones, he felt oddly elated and strangely serene. He finally knew who he was and where he belonged, and the knowledge was a tonic to his troubled soul. Having an identity, an awareness of self, an appreciation of his place in the cosmic scheme of things, anchored him to the here and now and gave him a purpose for living. His elation, however, was rudely shattered.

The door at the end of the hall unexpectedly opened, disgorging three Russian soldiers with AK-47's.

Chapter Sixteen

"What's the name of this town again, pard?"

"Strawberry Point," Geronimo answered.

"And how many folks lived there before the Big Blast?"

"According to the Atlas there were two thousand one hundred and twenty-nine."

"I doubt anyone lives there now," Marcus interjected.

"Cockroaches and rats, maybe," Hickok said, staring at the ghost town 200 yards from the idling SEAL. The buildings were in various stages of collapse. Roofs were partly gone or sagging. Walls were cracked and blistered. Windows were shattered, doors missing. Vegetation had reclaimed the yards; brush and trees grew where once tidy lawns had been meticulously cultivated.

"Where'd everybody go?" Marcus wondered aloud.

"We know the U.S. government evacuated hundreds of thousands of citizens during the war into the area now under the jurisdiction of the Civilized Zone," Geronimo mentioned. "Perhaps the people living in Strawberry Point were among those forced to relocate."

"Will we go around the town or straight through it?" Marcus asked.

Hickok pondered for a few seconds, then accelerated. "We've wasted too much blamed time as it is. We'll cut straight through."

Geronimo gazed to the right at a verdant field, then at the blue sky. In the distance, seemingly on the very horizon, hovered a dark speck, a large bird of some kind. He looked out the windshield at Strawberry Point, his brow knitting. Since when did birds hover? Few birds could hang stationary in the air. He glanced at the south again, studying the speck.

"What's that?" Marcus asked, pointing straight ahead.

Geronimo stared at the spot Marcus indicated, a spot well past Strawberry Point and several hundred feet above the ground, and he tensed when he spied another speck, only this one was slightly larger. He estimated the distance at over a mile, possibly two. Troubled by the fact there were two of the things, he twisted and checked the sky to their rear. And there, hovering far away, was a third speck. "Uh-oh," he said.

"What is it?" Hickok inquired.

"We've got trouble."

The gunman slowed the transport while scanning the town. "Where? What kind?"

"Look out your window and tell me if you see a big speck to the north," Geronimo suggested.

"A speck?" Hickok repeated quizzically. He searched the sky, then suddenly braked. "Yep. I see one."

"There's one on every side," Geronimo revealed.

"What are they?" Marcus queried, gazing from one dot to the next.

"They sure ain't gigantic hummingbirds," Hickok quipped.

"I wonder how long they've had us under surveillance," Geronimo commented.

"Who?" Marcus questioned.

"If they've been on our tail for a spell, it means we were set up," Hickok said.

"Who set us up?" Marcus asked.

"Maybe they found us by sheer luck," Geronimo stated. "Maybe they were on patrol and spotted the smoke from the barricade we destroyed or that car the grenade took out."

"Maybe," Hickok said, but his tone lacked conviction.

"Who found us? Will one of you tell me what's going on?" Marcus requested.

Hickok pointed at the speck to the east. "Commies."

"The Russians? But we're not in Russian territory," Marcus noted.

"We're in eastern Iowa, about fifty miles from the border," Geronimo said. "The next state over is Illinois, which the Russians control portions of. We're well within the patrol radius of a standard copter."

"So those specks are Russian choppers?" Marcus responded, and grinned. "All right! More action."

Hickok glanced at Geronimo. "Would you remind me to dunk him in the moat when we get back?"

"No problem. I'll even help."

"Thanks, pard."

"Hey, what's the big deal? We can handle a few helicopters," Marcus declared. "We've got the Stinger mounted on the roof, remember?"

"Correct, rocks for brains," Hickok replied. "We've got *one* surface-to-air missile. There are *four* helicopters."

"We can take them," Marcus predicted confidently.

"I hope so," Geronimo said, "because here they come."

The specks were rapidly growing larger and larger as the four helicopters converged on the SEAL, their spinning rotors and low, squat contours becoming visible within seconds.

Hickok floored it, bringing the transport up to 60 miles an hour, heading for Strawberry Point. He held off activating the Stinger, preferring to wait until the missile was really needed. Why waste his ace in the hole early on when they were about to fight tooth and nail against superior forces? He knew trying to elude the choppers in the trees would be next to impossible, and the dense vegetation would limit the SEAL's manueverability. Trying to outrun the helicopters would be equally ridiculous. So his sole option was to reach the town and try to reduce the approach angle the copters could employ by interposing buildings between the transport and the whirlybirds.

The Russian copters came on swiftly. Despite the distance they had to cover, they almost overtook the van before it could enter Strawberry Point.

Almost.

But not quite.

The Russian chopper speeding in from the east was only 100 yards off when Hickok steered the SEAL into the deserted town. He looked for a turnoff, a driveway, anything, uncomfortably conscious of the helicopter bearing down on them, expecting the brown craft to fire its rockets at any instant. To his astonishment, nothing happened.

With a loud whump-whump-whump the military craft shot over the SEAL and continued to the west.

"They didn't try to nail us," Marcus remarked in bewilderment.

Hickok spied an alley a block off on the right side of the highway, and he made for it without delay.

"Why didn't they open fire?" Marcus asked.

"Maybe they want to take the SEAL intact," Geronimo conjected, "or else they want us alive."

"They'll get us over my dead body," Hickok snapped, and jerked on the steering wheel as the transport arrived at the alley. The SEAL narrowly missed the building on the left and was 15 feet inside the alley before he slammed on the brakes. "Wait here," he directed them, shifting into Park. He grabbed the Henry from the console and quickly climbed from the van. Where were the Commies? he wondered. He anticipated the choppers would materialize over the alley in force, but ten seconds elapsed and they failed to appear although he could hear the sound of their rotors.

What the blazes was going on?

The gunman ran to the mouth of the alley and peered out. To the north, hovering several hundred yards from Strawberry Point, was one of the helicopters. He glanced over his right shoulder and found a second craft positioned to the south, likewise holding back. Why were the vermin waiting to attack?

Seconds later a third chopper appeared, this time off to the east at the far edge of town. The copter alighted in the center of the highway and sat there, its blades still spinning, apparently waiting.

For what? Hickok speculated.

The fourth helicopter suddenly swooped down to the west and landed just outside of Strawberry Point, its fuselage across the highway, not more than 60 yards away.

Hickok hefted the Henry, feeling frustrated. They were boxed in. He turned and motioned with his right arm at the transport, and moments later Geronimo and Marcus joined him.

"What are they doing?" Geronimo queried.

"Your guess is as good as mine," Hickok responded. "They have us hemmed in on all four sides."

"I vote we make a break for it," Marcus proposed.

"And if they won't move out of our way, we can ram them," Hickok said facetiously.

"Now you're talking," Marcus replied eagerly.

"We have company," Geronimo observed.

The gunfighter glanced at the helicopter to the west. A tall, lean man in the uniform of an officer, his chest decorated with ribbons, was stepping from the cabin, his shoulders hunched against the wind from the rotors, his hands holding his cap in place on his head. He advanced for 20 yards, then halted with his hands on his hips. "Warriors!" he bellowed. "We must talk."

"I'll go," Hickok said. "The two of you can cover my back."

"You shouldn't be the one to go," Geronimo remarked.

"Why not? I won't let the mangy polecat get the jump on me," Hickok promised.

"I doubt he speaks Martian."

The gunman glared at Geronimo, then slung the Henry over his left shoulder and ambled toward the Russian. He could see other soldiers in the helicopter, but they made no move to leave the craft.

The officer came forward to meet the Warrior halfway, his steps clipped and precise. His uniform was immaculate, his boots polished to a sheen. A square jaw contributed to the impression he conveyed of no-nonsense authority, a soldier of distinction and a man who wielded power dispassionately. "I am Major General Ligachev," he announced when he halted two yards from Hickok.

"Howdy. I'm the Lone Ranger."

Ligachev smirked and shook his head. "You are the Warrior called Hickok, are you not?"

The gunman's eyes narrowed. "How'd you know my name?"

"You were captured once and taken to Washington, D.C., where you were interrogated by Comrade General Malenkov," Ligachev went on, ignoring the question. "Unfortunately, you escaped."

"I'm partial to my freedom," Hickok said. "Besides, some of the folks there were a mite inhospitable."

"You are a close friend to the top Warrior, Blade. You were with him in Cincinnati when he destroyed our greatest scientific achievement, Lenin's Needle," Ligachev stated.

"That doohickey was an eyesore."

"You are en route now to Boston, where you hope to rescue Blade. How many are with you?"

Hickok didn't like the smug tone the officer was using. "You seem to know an awful lot about me," he commented.

"How many of your fellow Warriors are with you?" Major General Ligachev repeated.

"I've plumb forgotten. Ten or twenty, I reckon."

The officer gazed toward the alley, then at Hickok. "The number doesn't matter. All of you will surrender immediately. You will lay down your arms and step to the middle of the street with your hands overhead."

"Don't hold your breath."

Ligachev gestured at the helicopter to his rear. "I have four such aircraft at my disposal. Each one is armed with machine guns, rockets, and nose cannons. Your vaunted SEAL is formidable and durable, but your van can't withstand my little fleet.''

Hickok glanced at the chopper. "I reckon we can give you a run for your money."

"Be sensible," Ligachev said. "There is no way you will escape. Our trap has been too carefully planned. We have expended considerable time, energy, and expense to spring our surprise, and we have foreseen every contingency."

The Warrior studied the officer's cold green eyes and haughty countenance. "This was planned?"

"Of course, you moron," Major General Ligachev stated. "Allow me to elaborate so you will fully appreciate the extent of our genius and the folly of resisting us. As I noted, you are en route to Boston to try and save Blade, who was abducted slightly over a week ago while on his way back to the Home from Halma. Am I correct so far?"

Hickok merely nodded.

"Your accursed Family had no idea where the giant could be, although you did find signs of a struggle, until one of you discovered a matchbook," Ligachev related arrogantly. "Am I still correct?"

"You're a regular mind reader."

"I get better. Part of the matchbook cover was missing, but the matches clearly came from Sam's Bar in Boston, Massachusetts. Your Elders deciced to send a rescue mission, which explains your presence in this quaint town," Ligachev said.

Hickok wanted to bash his head against the nearest building. He felt like such a chump. "The matches were a plant."

Major General Ligachev chuckled. "The matches were a plant. Did you really believe one of our elite commando teams, the HGP Unit, no less, would be stupid enough to leave such incriminating evidence behind? We wanted you to find the matches. General Malenkov knew your Family would send Warriors to Blade's rescue. He predicted the SEAL would be used, and he arranged for our welcoming committee."

"But we're not even in Russian territory," Hickok said lamely.

"You will be by midnight," Ligachev stated. "We intended to spring our trap where you would least expect it, and you undoubtedly did not suspect we were in this area. Did you?"

"No," Hickok admitted.

"Actually, the SEAL has been under surveillance since one of my flight spotted a spiral of smoke earlier. You see, although we couldn't be certain of the exact route you would take, logic dictated you would travel in a relatively direct line because of the time factor, which in your estimation would be critical. It was no wondrous feat to calculate that you would cut across the northeast corner of Iowa. Since we already knew of your predilection for traveling on secondary roads as opposed to the major highways, all we had to do was fly a grid pattern over the northeast corner, concentrating on the secondary roads, until one of us spotted the SEAL. Then we simply reformed and sprang our trap," Ligachev related.

"But you couldn't have known what day we'd be comin' through," Hickok noted. He took a quirky delight in being able to criticize their meticulous plot.

"Which is why we have worked in six-hour shifts on a rotational basis. My flight is not the only one. There are three other flights of four copters apiece, and each of our flights pulls a six-hour shift daily. If we pulled a longer shift, we would expend our fuel and be unable to reach our base," Ligachev said. "We've been waiting for the SEAL for a week. Frankly, we expected you long before this."

"Glad we disappointed you."

"Now don't be petty," the officer stated testily. "You have nothing to be ashamed of. Our superior intellect was bound to prevail."

"Gee, I wish I was wearin' boots," Hickok quipped.

Major General Ligachev frowned. "Enough of this idle chatter. I have graciously explained more than was necessary."

"Why didn't you bozos just blow the SEAL to bits? Why go to all this trouble?" Hickok asked.

"Because General Malenkov gave specific orders to avoid damaging the SEAL, if possible. Your vehicle is quite unique, and our scientists and engineers could learn a lot by examining it. Be smart and lay down your weapons. Now.''

''And if we don't oblige?''

''Then we will reduce the SEAL to so much scrap. General Malenkov prefers the van in one piece, but he commanded us to obliterate it if you won't surrender,'' Ligachev stated, and looked meaningfully at the gunman. ''So don't be a fool. I want your answer, and I want it now. Will you hand over your weapons and the SEAL?''

Hickok glanced back at the alley, then at the chopper. He grinned and leaned forward slightly. ''I know all Russian soldiers are supposed to be able to speak Russian and English, right?''

Major General Ligachev squared his shoulders. ''All of our troops are bilingual. Why?''

''I want to be sure you'll get my drift when I give you our answer.''

''Which is?'' Ligachev snapped impatiently.

''Get stuffed.''

Chapter Seventeen

Blade executed a flying dive, his hands grabbing for the Falcon and the Beretta in midair. He came down hard on his elbows and knees, his body prone, and pointed the pistols at the three Soviet troopers.

The trio tried to bring their AK-47's to bear. Impulsively, the foremost Russian elevated his barrel and fired from the hip, the blasting of the AK-47 being added to the wail of the klaxons. In his haste he missed.

Blade squeezed off a shot from the Falcon in his right hand, and he saw the round catch the soldier between the eyes and send the man stumbling backwards into one of the other troopers. The unaffected soldier raised his AK-47 to his shoulder, apparently foolishly intending to take the time to aim, but in the interval of less than a second that it took him to lift the assault rifle, a slug from the Beretta bored into his brain and burst out the rear of his skull.

The second Russian dropped.

Leaving only the third, who had shoved the first man aside and was bringing his AK-47 to bear on the giant when the Falcon and the Beretta both boomed. As one, the twin shots ripped through the soldier's head and he spun around into the wall, then collapsed, leaving a crimson stain where his head made contact.

Blade heaved erect and sprinted to the three men. He wedged the pistols under his belt, then claimed two of the AK-47's for his own, slinging one over his left shoulder and cradling the other. Moving fast, he walked to the door, glanced at the small sign that read STAIRWELL, and shoved the door wide. He entered the stairwell and paused on the landing. The stairs continued upward, but there was no reason for him to ascend them. He started down at a brisk pace, taking three steps at a stride, thankful the blaring klaxons weren't as loud in the stairwell. Two floors passed without any problems arising, and then a Russian soldier appeared on the next landing, hastening toward the Warrior.

The trooper's eyes were on the steps.

Blade halted and leveled the AK-47. "Freeze," he barked.

Startled, the Russian looked up. He made a desperate attempt to train his AK-47 on the giant.

The Warrior sent a short burst into the soldier's chest, and the impact hurled the man rearward to crash onto the landing with his arms outflung. The trooper's AK-47 sailed over the edge of the landing and plummeted to the bottom of the stairwell, clattering noisily when it hit the bottom.

Blade took the steps four at a time now, dominated by an urgent feeling to get well clear of the hospital before more reinforcements than he could handle arrived. He grinned when he saw the final landing below, and he dashed to the door and pressed his left ear to the panel.

Just as someone barreled into the door from the far side.

The door struck the Warrior in the temple and he threw his left forearm against it in sheer reflex, stopping its movement.

"What the hell!" someone blurted out on the other side.

Blade grabbed the edge and heaved, yanking the door open as he side stepped, aiming the AK-47 at the stocky figure in front of him.

Another Soviet soldier, a young officer armed with a pistol in a holster on his right hip, gaped at the giant. "You!" he cried.

"Me," Blade said, and blasted the Russian at near point-blank range. The man crumpled in a disjointed heap.

Somewhere a woman screamed.

The Warrior stepped over the officer and hurried down the corridor. Unlike the sixth floor, this floor was crammed with people: nurses, doctors, patients, visitors, and other hospital staff, most of whom decided to make themselves scarce. They darted into rooms and slammed the doors. Those too scared or astonished to gather their wits simply flattened against the wall and watched him with wide eyes.

A man dressed in a white smock, a notebook in his left hand, stood his ground defiantly in the center of the hall and blocked the Warrior's path. "Who the hell are you?" he demanded angrily. "What do you think you're doing? You're not going anywhere!"

"Bet me," Blade responded, and planted his left fist on the man's mouth. Teeth crunched, blood gushed from flattened lips, and the fool tottered rearward and fell, whining and gurgling.

A different woman screeched in terror.

Blade increased his speed, running as fast as he could, dodging people, carts, and wheelchairs. Thirty feet ahead he spied glass doors. Beyond the doors, beckoning him with the implied promise of freedom and hope, was sunlight.

A nurse built like a tank, over six feet in height and almost as wide, endeavored to intercept him. She moved to the doors and faced him with her hands on her broad hips. "Stop!" she shouted.

The Warrior slowed and motioned for her to step out of the way.

"You're not leaving, you son of a bitch!" she growled. Then, incredibly, she charged him.

Blade shifted the AK-47 to his left hand and halted, his right fist clenching tightly, amazed at her behavior, amazed that an unarmed nurse would needlessly risk her life trying to stop him. Unless, as with Milton and Krittenbauer, the nurse wasn't as she seemed.

She assumed a boxing posture and waded into him swinging, her punches controlled and demonstrating a practiced rhythm.

Successfully dodging the first few blows, Blade was jarred by a clip on his jaw. He set himself and retaliated with a sweeping right to her nose.

The nurse clutched at her face and straightened, roaring in pain but still on her feet.

Blade frowned and went to skirt her, but her right hand flicked out and snagged his right forearm. Seething at the delay, he gripped the AK-47 and whipped the stock into her head with all of his might. She let go and wobbled to the right, her eyes fluttering. He promptly raced to the glass doors and pushed through to the outside, blinking in the bright sunshine, and inhaled the odorous city air gratefully.

He was out!

Below the concrete steps leading to Kruschev Memorial, running from north to south, was a bustling street packed with pedestrians and traffic. A few of the passersby stopped to gawk at him as he emerged, but the majority were too involved in their own affairs to pay him much attention.

That all changed a moment later.

Blade headed for the sidewalk, and he was only halfway down the steps when a man attired in a blue uniform, a policeman, materialized off to the right.

The policeman took one look and clawed at his service revolver. "You there! Halt!" he yelled.

Growing increasingly perturbed by the constant obstacles to his escape, Blade crouched and swung the AK-47 around to bear on the officer. "Don't!" Blade warned, but his shout went unheeded. He saw the service revolver begin to clear the holster and he squeezed the trigger. The AK-47 chattered and a half-dozen rounds thwacked into the policeman and flattened him on the spot.

Pedestrians shrieked and clamored in alarm. They pushed and jostled one another in their haste to vacate the vicinity of the concrete steps.

Blade cleared the remaining steps in three leaps and alighted on the sidewalk. The traffic in the street flowed at a slow pace because of the congestion and the fact that a few of the drivers had witnessed the death of the policeman and then braked to stare at the Warrior in dumbfounded shock. Off to the north a siren blared, and Blade could see a flashing red light in the distance, coming closer rapidly.

He needed to get out of there!

But which way?

Instinct more than anything else made him suddenly whirl toward the hospital entrance. He hadn't heard any unusual sounds. He hadn't detected any motion out of the corners of his eyes. He simply sensed that there were adversaries to his rear and the short hairs at the nape of his neck prickled his skin. His instincts served him in good stead.

Coming through the glass doors were four soldiers. The foremost trooper opened fire the instant he stepped into the sunshine.

Blade threw himself to the left and bruised his elbows on the concrete when he landed. A hail of lead zipped through the space he'd just occupied and pinged into a car parked at the curb. He tilted the AK-47 upward and cut loose. Hit in the torso and flung rearward, the foremost trooper smashed into the glass doors and dropped.

Undaunted, the three remaining soldiers joined in the battle.

Blade knew they would slay him within seconds if he stayed put, so he moved, he moved to the right, reversing direction, rolling over and over, keeping his body always on the go. If he stopped he was dead. So he rolled and rolled with the bullets striking the sidewalk all around him until he came to the end of the steps and a stone wall three feet in height temporarily sheltered him from the troopers. He rose to his knees, astonished he didn't have so much as a scratch, and aimed at the three soldiers, who were rushing down the stairs toward the wall. One of them snapped off a few hasty rounds, and then Blade fired a substained burst, sweeping the AK-47 from right to left, mowing the trio down. They thrashed and convulsed as the rounds perforated their bodies, and one of them vented a scream of primal terror at his demise.

Move! Blade's mind urged.

The Warrior rose and stepped to the curb. The flashing red light to the north was much nearer. He scanned the cars and trucks in the street, most of which had braked, the drivers regarding him in horror as if he was some kind of monster.

A yellow vehicle caught his eye.

Twenty-five feet to the south, stuck between a cement truck, was a bright yellow car, looking as if it had been recently washed and waxed. On the doors were the words YELLOW CAB, on the roof a plastic sign bearing the word TAXI. The vehicle attracted Blade's attention for three reasons. First, there was only one occupant, a portly man behind the wheel. Second, the yellow car was somewhat smaller than most of the cars in sight. Third, and most important, eight feet separated the cement truck from the taxi.

More than enough space.

Blade ran to the south, then cut between the cab and the black sedan behind it. He walked warily to the driver's door and poked the barrel of the AK-47 in the open window. "Out of the car," he commanded.

The heavyset driver, who had been about to talk into a square microphone in his right hand, looked around and gasped. His jowly features quivered and his brown eyes became four times their normal size. "What?" he asked in disbelief.

"Out of the car," Blade repeated.

"What for?" the driver asked anxiously.

Blade yanked the door open. "I don't have time to explain. Out. Now." To his surprise, the man mustered the courage to refuse.

"No way, mister. This is a company cab. If you wreck it, they'll dock my pay. I've got six mouths to feed."

The Warrior glanced to the north. The red light was several hundred yards off.

"So go ahead and shoot," the taxi driver was saying. "Or pound me to a pulp if you want. But I'm not turning this cab over to you.''

Blade frowned and moved to haul the man from the cab.

''I can drive you wherever you need to go,'' the driver said quickly. ''I can always tell the police you forced me to take you.''

''Drive me?'' the Warrior stated, and the idea appealed to him. He slammed the door shut and dashed around the front of the cab, the AK-47 trained on the driver with every stride, and slid in the passenger side.

The man licked his thick lips and blanched. ''What are you doing?''

''You wanted to drive,'' Blade said. ''Start driving.''

''Me and my big mouth,'' the man muttered. He slid the microphone into a slot on the dash and looked at the cement truck. ''Where am I supposed to go? The traffic is standing still.''

''Use the sidewalk.''

''The sidewalk? You're kidding.''

Blade jammed the barrel into the man's side to demonstrate his sincerity.

''Okay. Okay. I can take a hint,'' the driver declared, and smiled wanly. ''My name is Harold. What's yours?''

''Drive,'' Blade ordered harshly.

''Anyone ever tell you that you have a one-track mind?'' Harold asked. The AK-47 dug deeper into his ribs. He looked down, gulped, and pressed on the gas, angling the cab to the right, onto the sidewalk, the tires bumping over the curb. He drove between the cement truck on the left and a wall on the right, the cab barely negotiating the narrow gap. Ahead were more vehicles, eight or nine, stopped in the street, the drivers all staring back at the hospital. Pedestrians on the sidewalk scurried for cover.

Blade spied an alley on his side, less than 50 feet off. ''Into the alley.''

''It's one way. It's illegal to enter from this direction.''

''*The alley!*''

Harold glanced at the giant. ''Hey, you want to go down the

alley, we'll go down the damn alley. I learned a long time ago not to mess with guys who can bench-press a skyscraper."

"You wouldn't let me take the cab," Blade noted, constantly scrutinizing the street, the sidewalk, and the nearby buildings.

"I told you why. If you damage this cab, the bastards will make me pay for the damages. I can hardly feed my family as it is. If they take any more money out of my pay, we'll be out on the streets."

"You're devoted to your family?"

"Sure. Why the hell wouldn't I be?"

"Die-hard communists don't believe in the sanctity of the family," Blade mentioned to test the driver's loyalties. "Karl Marx wanted the family abolished."

Harold's lips compressed. He concentrated on the alley, and waited until he performed the turn before responding. "I can't believe you're a KGB agent."

"I'm not."

"You never know. The bastards are everywhere," Harold stated.

"I get that impression."

"You don't look like a run-of-the-mill criminal," Harold mentioned.

"I'm not."

"Who are you? Where are you from?"

"I'm from outside the Soviet territory."

"Outside!" Harold exclaimed, flabbergasted. In his excitement he inadvertently caused the cab to swerve to the left, almost colliding with the rear wall of a brick building.

"How long have you been driving?" Blade quipped, hoping the conversation might help the man to relax. His goal would be achieved much sooner if he could persuade Harold to assist him, wittingly or not.

"Are you really from the Outlands?"

"I never said the Outlands. I'm from ouside the Soviet-controlled territory. That's all I can tell you."

"I'll be damned," Harold said. He braked as they came to the end of the alley and stared at the intersecting street. "I've

never met anyone from the outside. All I've heard are stories."
A break in the trafffic flow permitted him to pull out, and he
took a sharp right, nervously scanning the street for police cars.
"What's it like out there?"

"I'll ask the questions."

"Oh. Sorry."

"First things first. Do you know where Gorbachev Air Force
Base is located?"

"The old Hanscom Air Force Base? Sure. It's about fifteen,
maybe twenty miles from here."

"Take me there," Blade directed.

"Okay."

Blade reached out and tapped the microphone. "What do you
use this for?"

"To keep in touch with the dispatcher. If somebody needs
a cab, they'll phone the company and the dispatcher will tell
me where to pick up the fare," Harold explained, and chuckled.
"Haven't you ever ridden in a cab before?" he asked in jest.

"No."

Harold did a double take. "You're putting me on."

"Can your dispatcher monitor the cab in any way?"

"How do you mean?"

"Does the dispatcher know where you are at any given
moment?"

"No, man. It's just a two-way radio, is all. Like a CB. You've
used a CB before, haven't you?"

"No."

Harold looked at the giant. "Where *are* you from? The
moon?"

Blade smiled. He twisted and gazed out the rear window,
checking for pursuit. "Life outside the Soviet zone is much
different. Except for a few organized factions, the standard of
livng is about the same as it was during the Middle Ages.
Functional cars and trucks are rare. Indoor plumbing is a luxury.
The people are lucky if they eat one square meal a day." He
paused. "Ironically, the standard of living in the Soviet territory
is more like the life-style in the prewar United States than that

in amost every other area, despite the Communist system the Russians have tried to impose.''

"I get the impression you know a lot about the Soviets."

"I've dealt with them before."

A voice suddenly squawked from a small speaker. "Fifty-four. Pick up a woman wearing a green dress at the corner of Harvard Street and Walk Hill."

"That's me," Harold said.

"Ignore it."

The speaker crackled again. "Fifty-four. Are you alive? Did you copy?"

"Boy, will he be ticked off," Harold remarked, and twisted a dial to kill the speaker.

"How much trouble will you get into for driving me to the base?" Blade inquired.

"Not much. I saw what you did at the hospital, and I was about to let the dispatcher know I was stuck there when you commandeered my cab. The police will believe me when I tell them I didn't have a choice. I don't think they'll punish me," Harold said.

"Good."

Harold looked at the giant. "Say, do you mind if I ask you a question?"

"Not at all."

"Why, exactly, do you want to go to Gorbachev Air Force Base? You're on the run, aren't you? The authorities are after you. Going there doesn't make sense. There are military types all over the place."

"I know."

"Then why go there?" Harold queried, and the giant's reply almost prompted him to tramp on the brake.

"I plan to attack it."

Chapter Eighteen

Major General Ligachev wheeled and took a step.

"Now don't go off in a huff," Hickok said. "We need to shoot the breeze a bit."

The officer turned, the set of his features revealing his anger. "I have nothing left to say to you. Surrender, or else."

The Warrior gazed at the helicopter at rest to the west. The troopers inside were still seated, their AK-47's in their laps or held in their hands. None of them were aiming a weapon at him. "Maybe I was a mite hasty."

"What?"

"I reckon a surrender is in order."

Ligachev nodded and smirked. "You finally see the light. There is no way you can escape us. Resistance would be futile."

Hickok hooked his thumbs in his gunbelt. "Yep, you coyotes sure have this all thought out. But there's a few things I don't understand."

"Such as?"

"Why didn't you guys track the SEAL from the Home? It would have been a lot simpler."

"True," the officer acknowledged, "But had we attempted to shadow your vehicle all the way from the Home, we increased the likelihood of being detected."

"Why'd you spring your trap now? Why not earlier? Or why not later?"

"Our fuel consumption was a major factor in our decision. Any earlier and we would have been too far from our lines to be able to engage you, if you refused to give in, and still have enough fuel left to return to our refueling site. Our helicopters haven't been modified to fly extended distances, like the one the HGP Unit used to fly to the Home. Such modifications are expensive, and only a few such craft have been converted," Ligachev said. "We could have waited until later, but we ran the risk of not being able to find the SEAL. There are few secondary roads in this section of Iowa, making the area ideal. And as General Malenkov said, the sooner the better."

"How is old cow face?"

"Eager to see you," Ligachev responded, and grinned wickedly.

"I'll bet," Hickok stated. He allowed his hands to slowly drop to his sides. "I've got one last point that's puzzlin' me. Malenkov wants the Home destroyed. He hates our guts. So why'd he send in the commandos just to snatch Blade? Why not send them in to blow up the Home?"

"That's been tried before without success. Your compound even withstood a direct assault by a vastly superior force during your war with the Docktor. Before the general sends his elite unit against the Home, he wants to learn all about your defenses. He wants to know everything there is to know about your compound. That's one of the reasons Blade was taken," Major General Ligachev detailed. "You are right about the general hating your Family. After he is done, your compound will be reduced to rubble and your Family will be dead or in prison. The general rates the destruction of the Home as his paramount priority, and he is giving the matter his personal touch."

Hickok nodded. "I guess that's all I need to know. It's time to surrender."

Ligachev extended his hands. "I'll take your weapons now."

"You've got it backwards, turkey."

"What?"

"I'm givin' *you* a chance to surrender."

"You're giving *us*—!" the officer exclaimed incredulously.

"Have your men line up behind you with their arms in the air," Hickok instructed him.

"You're insane."

"I mean every word I say."

Scarlet flushed the Russian's cheeks. "You've been toying with me. You had no serious intention of surrendering."

"You're the one who should give up before you get me riled."

Ligachev uttered a hissing noise and pivoted on his heel. He stalked toward the helicopter.

"Hey," Hickok said.

"What is it *now*?" the officer snapped, stopping and glancing at the Warrior.

"Do I take it your answer is no?"

"We'll never surrender to you, you dimwit," Ligachev said. "Once I give the word, your SEAL won't last two minutes."

The corners of Hickok's mustache curled upward. "You won't be givin' the word."

Major General Ligachev studied the man in buckskins, and the full meaning of the Warrior's words dawned. He glanced at the Colt Pythons, their pearl grips glistening in the sunshine, and remembered the many tales he had heard about the gunfighter's prowess. "Now wait a minute."

"Surrender, or else," Hickok said, mimicking the officer.

"If you shoot me, my men will slay you."

"Maybe. Maybe not."

Ligachev gestured at his waist. "But I'm unarmed. You can't shoot an unarmed man."

Hickok's forehead creased. "Why not?"

The unexpected question gave Ligachev pause. Why not, indeed? He'd executed dozens of unarmed political prisoners during his early years in the army. He cursed himself for being a fool, for not carrying a gun. "I came over here unarmed to show I only wanted to talk, to prove my good intentions."

"Good intentions? You're fixin' to blow us to bits."

Ligachev frantically thought of another argument he could use. "Killing me won't accomplish anything. My second-in-command will take over and the choppers will still destroy the SEAL."

"Pluggin' you will buy us a minute or two while your boys get their acts together," Hickok said. "I may rattle 'em so bad that they'll make mistakes."

Major General Ligachev began to back toward the helicopter. "Listen to me. I was told that Warriors are men of honor. How can you slay me in cold blood? Don't you have any morals?"

"I do have this code I live by," the gunman admitted.

Ligachev smiled. "There. See?"

"It's called do unto others before they do unto me," Hickok said, and drew. The Magnums streaked from their holsters and cracked in unison. The officer's eyes disappeared and the back of his head exploded outward.

Major General Ligachev died on his feet.

Hickok spun as the Russian started to crumple. He holstered the Colts and raced toward the alley, unslinging the Henry as he ran. Shouts sounded to his rear and he glanced over his left shoulder to see Soviet soldiers pouring from the helicopter. He looked at the mouth of the alley but saw no signs of Geronimo and Marcus. Where the blazes were they?

"Kill the son of a bitch!" someone bellowed gruffly from near the chopper.

Hickok heard the chatter of AK-47's and he weaved, never running in a straight line for more than a few yards. Rounds smacked into the asphalt or buzzed by. He felt a stinging twinge in his left shoulder and glanced down to see that he'd been nicked. Fifteen yards separated him from the alley, and he knew the Russians were bound to bring him down before he could reach it if Geronimo and Marcus didn't provide cover fire.

Where *were* they?

A high-pitched whine emanated from the alley and the SEAL

hurtled onto the highway, speeding in reverse. The van screeched to a halt, then rocketed in the gunman's direction.

Grinning, Hickok whirled and crouched, pressing the Henry to his right shoulder. He took a bead on a soldier leading the pack of Russians and fired, gratified when the soldier reacted as if a sledgehammer had pounded the trooper in the forehead. He snapped off a second shot, flattening another Russian, and then the SEAL braked abruptly alongside him and the passenger door was flung open.

"Need a lift?" Geronimo yelled.

The gunman vaulted onto the bucket seat and closed the door. "I thought you wanted me to do all the driving."

Geronimo drove forward, directly at the Russians. Bullets were striking the SEAL and ricocheting off. "I knew you'd pull a stupid stunt like this." His hands were glued to the steering wheel, his knuckles white.

"Like what?"

"I knew you'd blow that officer away," Geronimo said. "I figured you could use a little help."

Hickok smiled at his friend. "Thanks, pard."

They were closing rapidly on the Soviets. Geronimo pressed one of the toggle switches and the 50-caliber machine guns cut loose, their heavy slugs tearing the soldiers to ribbons. He kept the transport on a steady course, kept the machine guns belching lead, narrowing the range to the chopper. A hail of high—powered rounds hit the helicopter broadside, slaying a Russian who was trying to close the bay door. Geronimo angled the SEAL at the copter cockpit and the 50-calibers tracked accordingly, drilling into the cockpit, shattering it, exposing the pilot and copilot. Both were slain the next moment, punctured repeatedly. Geronimo switched off the machine guns. He made a tight U-turn, heading into the town again. "That helicopter won't get airborne again," he commented.

But the three others were already aloft and converging on the SEAL.

"Here they come," Hickok said.

The helicopter swooping in from the north and the one from

the south drew close together above Highway Three, their cockpits slanted at the SEAL.

"They're aimin' to use their nose cannons," Hickok declared, and he reached across the console to flick the toggle activating the Stinger.

At a distance of less than 50 yards, the streamlined missile was on the Russian craft before the pilots could so much as blink, let alone attempt evasive maneuvers. The Stinger struck the chopper on the north side of the highway and the resultant blast was tremendous. A billowing fireball consumed the first helicopter, then swirled outward and enshrouded the whirlybird hovering only a few dozen yards to the south. A second explosion shattered the heavens and rocked the buildings in Strawberry Point, and the added heat and gas and force produced a cumulative effect, creating a small sun, a brilliant ball of candescent energy that scorched the structures and ground underneath.

Geronimo applied the brakes and the transport lurched to a sudden stop. The SEAL was buffeted violently by the twin blasts, and even through the impervious shell the Warriors felt the heat.

"Wow!" Marcus exclaimed.

Intense but short-lived, the fireball dissipated swiftly. Debris rained on Strawberry Point. Twisted, smoldering wreckage and fried body parts thudded onto the highway and the roofs.

Hickok leaned forward, searching for the fourth helicopter, the one that had landed far off at the east end of town. Reddish-orange flames and plumes of black smoke obscured his view for over a minute. He finally caught sight of the ribbon of highway stretching into the distance, and tensed.

The last chopper was gone.

"Get this buggy movin'," Hickok urged.

Geronimo drove eastward, adroitly avoiding the larger segments of wreckage scattered in their path.

"Where'd the other helicopter go?" Marcus asked.

"Your guess is as good as mine," Hickok responded.

"Maybe it's on its way back to the Russian lines," Marcus said.

"I doubt it."

"Why? We just took out the other three. The Russians in the fourth helicopter won't want to mess with us."

"They'll come at us with everything they've got for the same reason I would if I was in their shoes," Hickok stated.

"What's that?"

"To get even."

They rode in silence for several hundred yards, their eyes on the sky.

"What are they waiting for?" Marcus queried impatiently.

"My guess is that they don't know we only had one stinger mounted on the roof," Geronimo said. "They don't want to suffer the same fate as their buddies, so they'll come in fast and low."

They did.

Like an enormous bird of prey, the Russian helicopter swept on the transport from out of the south, flying only a few yards above the trees and the rooftops.

Hickok glimpsed the chopper out of the corner of his right eye and swung around, crying in warning, "This side! Look out!" He saw a tiny puff of white smoke appear underneath the fuselage.

The roadway in front of the SEAL suddenly exploded, spraying chunks of asphalt and dirt in all directions.

Geronimo jerked on the steering wheel, cutting the van to the right, hanging onto the wheel tightly as the concussion from the blast hit the SEAL. He straightened the vehicle and scanned the sky for the enemy aircraft.

But the chopper had already vanished to the north.

"Hit and run," Hickok said bitterly. "Whatever you do, don't stop. We'll be sittin' ducks."

"Maybe we can lose it by hiding in an alley," Geronimo suggested.

"Get us out in the open where we can maneuver," Hickok

said. "Then we'll teach those hombres a lesson."

Geronimo angled the SEAL closer to the curb on the north side of the highway, using the structures bordering the road as partial cover. "How can we fight back? The machine guns, the rocket, and the flamethrower are all aligned to take care of targets directly in front of the SEAL."

"I'll think of something," Hickok replied.

"I was afraid you'd say that."

Two hundred yards passed and the helicopter failed to attack.

"Maybe they've given up," Marcus remarked.

Its rotors spinning and shimmering, the great brown craft came at them from out of the north, flying low as before. They fired another rocket.

Hickok grabbed the dashboard as a section of sidewalk to the south blew up, spewing concrete skyward. He kept his eyes on the helicopter, tracking the chopper as it flashed overhead and flew to the south. "Blast!"

"Sooner or later they'll nail us," Geronimo said.

"Too bad we can't ram 'em," Hickok responded. He scrutinized the highway ahead and spotted a huge building off to the left, perhaps an abandoned warehouse or a factory. Gigantic metal double doors hung wide, disclosing a gloomy interior. "Drive in there," he instructed.

Without an instant's hesitation Geronimo complied, steering deep into the bowels of the building, bypassing stacks of crates and cartons, and abruptly braked. "What now?"

"Everybody out," Hickok said, and shoved his door open. He jumped to the cement floor, cradled the Henry, and sprinted toward the metal doors. He spied a pile of metal drums along the right-hand wall.

Geronimo and Marcus raced on the gunman's heels.

"What are we doing?" Marcus asked.

"Hickok has a clever plan," Geronimo said. "Don't you, Nathan?"

"Nope," the gunfighter answered. "I'm wingin' it."

Geronimo looked at Marcus. "I trust you've made out your will?"

Hickok led them to the right and up to the corrugated metal wall, near the double doors. He placed his back to the wall and inched to the edge, then peered out. There was no sign of the Russian helicopter.

Yet.

"We've lost it for the time being," Hickok said.

"They'll figure out where we are eventually," Geronimo commented.

The gunman glanced at his friend. "Why do you always look on the bright side of things?"

Geronimo shrugged. "Just habit, I guess."

"Spread out," Hickok stated. "Check this whole place and let me know what you find."

"What are we hunting for?" Marcus wanted to know.

"I'll know that when we find it," Hickok replied, and darted away from the sunlight, into the building, making for the left side, inspecting every item he found. There was a lot of litter and trash. In one spot he found a heap of old tires. Elsewhere he came across a mound of cinder blocks, once apparently arranged in a tidy stack, now lying in a jumble. He also discovered more crates and disintegrating cardboard boxes.

From outside, from far away, arose the muted sound of the helicopter's rotors. The Russians were searching for them.

Hickok returned to the front of the warehouse where Geronimo and Marcus awaited him. "Well?"

"I found a lot of boxes, some chairs, and lumber," Marcus detailed.

"What kind of lumber?"

"Oh, planks, boards, a few shorter pieces."

"Is the wood rotten or sturdy?"

"I didn't test it," Marcus said.

"See if you can find me two sturdy boards about six feet in length and two feet wide," Hickok ordered.

"On my way," Marcus responded and hastened off.

The gunman faced Geronimo. "What about you?"

"Crates containing nails. Cartons containing cans of paint. A half-dozen antique washing machines. And metal strands of some sort.''

Hickok's interest was piqued. ''Metal stands?''

''Yeah. I have no idea what they were used for. They're flat on the bottom and the upper part slants to a peak.''

''How high are they?''

''I'd say a foot and a half at the most.''

''Go get a couple.''

Geronimo nodded and jogged into the depths of the structure.

An idea was forming in the gunfighter's mind, an elaborate ruse to lure the Russians into an ambush. He moved to the doorway and listened but couldn't hear the chopper. Good. The Russians were undoubtedly puzzled by the disappearance of the SEAL, and they were likely scouring the highway to the east, mistakenly thinking that the van was speeding from Strawberry Point. Their mistake. He wheeled and hurried to the metal drums he'd observed earlier. They turned out to be empty. After slinging the Henry over his left shoulder, he proceeded to roll one of the drums to the front of the warehouse. Back he went for another, and by the time he had three of them positioned in a line extending from the right-hand door across the doorway, Geronimo and Marcus came back bearing the items he'd requested.

''Where do you want these boards?'' Marcus inquired. He had hauled a pair of seven-foot-long boards, each three inches thick and two and a half feet wide, to the entrance. The exertion had hardly fazed him.

''Lay them right there,'' Hickok said, and Marcus complied.

Geronimo deposited the two strange metal stands. ''What next, fearless leader?''

The gunman nodded in the general direction of the cinder blocks. ''There's a bunch of heavy blocks back that-a-way. I don't know how many I'll need yet, so lug about six of them over here.''

Geronimo and Marcus began to walk off.

''Not you, Marcus,'' Hickok said. ''You can lend me a hand with the drums.''

''How many do you want?''

"Enough to make a wall."

"A wall?"

"You'll see," Hickok stated.

Together they carted fifteen more metal drums to the front and stacked them three high and six across, constructing a makeshift wall.

"We'll need six more," Hickok declared after gazing at the SEAL.

Yet another layer was added to the top. Geronimo finished with the cinder blocks and assisted in carrying the last drum.

"That ought to do it," Hickok said, surveying their handiwork critically.

"Do what? That dinky wall won't stop the copter," Marcus noted.

"It's not supposed to stop that overgrown dragonfly," Hickok stated. He looked at Geronimo. "Would you drive the buggy on over here, pard?"

"No problem."

The gunman motioned at Marcus. "Give me a hand with these boards and the rest."

Working rapidly under Hickok's guidance, the two Warriors placed the metal stands six feet from the wall of gray drums, positioning the stands about ten feet apart. Then they aligned three cinder blocks in a row behind each of the stands, leaving a foot of space between each block.

Marcus studied the arrangement and snickered. "What in the world are you doing?"

"I'm not done yet," Hickok said, and picked up the first board. He carefully set the end of the board on top of the left metal stand and positioned the full length over the cinder blocks, then set the board down. He repeated the procedure on the right side.

Perplexed, Marcus scratched his head. They had fabricated a crude ramp with the high end near the makeshift wall of drums. He could see that much. But he still didn't comprehend how the wall and the ramp would enable them to defeat the last helicopter. "Care to explain what you intend to do?"

"In a bit," Hickok replied. He stood next to the metal drums and watched the SEAL approach at a crawl. Motioning with his arms, he directed Geronimo, insuring the transport's tires were perfectly in line with the board.

Marcus glanced from the board to the SEAL and back again. His eyes widened and he looked at the gunman. "I get it! But those boards will never support the entire weight of the SEAL."

"They only have to support the front end," Hickok said, crossing his fingers. He beckoned Geronimo onward.

The van crept forward until the tires touched the lower edges of the boards.

Geronimo poked his head out of the SEAL. "How am I doing?"

"Just fine," Hickok said. "Take it real slow and easy. I'll let you know when to stop. And hurry. That chopper will return soon." He riveted his gaze on the boards as the transport crawled onto the ramp. Please hold! he prayed. The boards creaked and sagged, but they didn't break. He measured the progress mentally, scarcely breathing, anxious to dispose of the Russians so they could go to the aid of Blade.

One inch.

Two.

Four.

At five inches the boards sagged even more, but they still held.

Six.

Seven.

Nine.

Hickok gestured for Geronimo to stop, then walked around to the driver's side. "Nice job."

"As a certain friend of mine is so fond of saying, it was a piece of cake," Geronimo said.

"Sit tight and wait for Marcus to give you the signal to fire the rocket."

Geronimo stared at the wall of metal drums. "But those things are blocking my view. How can I fire the rocket if I can't see the target?"

"You let me worry about that," Hickok replied. "Just be ready."

"What are you going to do?"

Hickok ignored the question and stepped to the drum wall. He looked at the SEAL, at the middle of the front grill where the secret compartment housing the rocket was located, then envisioned the trajectory the rocket would need. He removed two of the drums from the center and pulled them aside. Now the SEAL had a clear shot at the airspace just outside the warehouse. "Marcus."

"Yeah?"

"Stand here and keep a watch. When the chopper gets within thirty feet of the front of this building, when you think the angle is right, signal Geronimo to fire."

The gladiator came over. "I doubt the pilot will fly the helicopter so close."

"You let me worry about that," Hickok said, and stepped to the left of his improvised wall.

"What are you planning to do?" Marcus said, echoing Geronimo's question.

Again the gunfighter ignored the query. "Be ready," he ordered, and darted into the open, making for the middle of the highway. He looked back at the warehouse, assessing the trap. The drum wall effectively screened the SEAL from any casual scrutiny, although the grill was visible where he had removed the two drums. Now everything depended on him luring the whirlybird into position. The ramp had elevated the transport enough so the rocket would speed on a slight trajectory. Not much of a trajectory, granted, but it would have to do the job.

Now where the blazes were the Russians?

Hickok slowed and strolled to the faded yellow center line. He surveyed the horizon in every direction. If the pilot had flown to the east after the SEAL, then the helicopter should return shortly. He unslung the Henry and walked eastward, his nerves on edge, feeling exposed and terribly vulnerable. A rifle and a pair of revolvers were no match for the flying arsenal.

Several minutes elapsed.

The Warrior halted and gazed at the warehouse, deciding he'd gone far enough. All he could do was wait.

And wait.

Hickok began to wonder if the Russians had called it quits and flown toward their lines. Why else would they be taking so long? He sighed and stared to the south.

The helicopter came at him from the north.

One moment he was alone, the breeze on his cheeks, the sun warming his skin, and the next an aerial demon rushed out of the blue, zeroing in on him, its machine guns blazing.

To Hickok the sound of the machine guns resembled the din of thunder. He inadvertently flinched and crouched, shielding his face with his arms as the highway was stitched to the right and the left by the powerful rounds, the shots missing him by inches. In the space of seconds the chopper was past him and flying to the south. He spun and raced for the warehouse, following the copter with his eyes, watching the pilot execute a wide loop and swing back toward the town.

Toward him.

He covered ten yards and saw the familiar puffs of smoke under the fuselage. His arms outflung, he dived for the ground. A volcano seemed to flare into life at the very spot he'd vacated, and he was pelted with bruising fragments of the road.

The helicopter arced overhead.

Hickok pushed himself up and ran for his life, his moccasins pounding hard on the asphalt, his heart pounding even harder, his ears ringing from the explosions.

This time the chopper swung to the west and banked, zooming at him once more, soaring over the warehouse. The pilot tilted the craft for a better view.

In desperation Hickok threw the Henry to his shoulder and banged off three shots, working the lever as fast as he could, aiming at the cockpit. He must have struck it too, because the helicopter slanted to the south a few dozen feet, which wasn't enough to interfere with the pilot's aim.

The nose cannons boomed.

The Warrior flattened and hugged the roadway, his left cheek scraping on the rough surface, and he thought of his wife and son as an earthquake caused the earth around him to buck and heave. Dirt and dust cascaded upon him. He heard the copter fly to the east.

Go! Go! Go!

The word screamed over and over again in his mind as he rose and sprinted toward those inviting double doors, toward the makeshift wall, toward the friends he might never see again. The hair at the nape of his neck prickled and he imagined the Russian pilot closing the distance swiftly, the machine guns set to fire. He zigzagged, expecting bursts that never came. Confused, he glanced over his right shoulder and nearly tripped over his own feet.

A ten-ton arrow whizzed at him, the chopper almost skimming the highway. In clear sight in the cockpit, beaming maliciously, sat the enemy pilot. His intent was obvious.

Hickok stopped, stunned. The prick was going to ram him, to bowl him over and reduce him to so much crimson-soaked pulp! Enraged, he managed to squeeze off a single shot and dropped prone for a third time. A vortex of wind pummeled his back, causing the fringe of his buckskins to flap wildly. He peered skyward and saw the underbelly of the craft streak by within two feet of his head. Every nut and bolt was visible. He could have sworn he heard mocking laughter. But that was impossible.

The helicopter rose and flew to the south, performing a circular maneuver.

This was it!

Licking his lips, Hickok leaned erect and dashed all out for the warehouse. He had to be in the proper position, directly in front of the double doors, when the chopper reached him. Any mistakes now meant certain death. The Russians had missed him three times; evading them a fourth time would be extremely unlikely. Unless, as he suspected, they were toying with him.

The copter came toward the gunman at a leisurely speed, the

pilot apparently convinced he had the Warrior dead to rights.

Hickok reached a point in the middle of Highway Three and 20 yards from the wall of gray drums. He faced the chopper, appalled to discover the craft hovering at least ten yards too far to the west.

Blast!

The Warrior sighted the Henry on the cockpit and squeezed off a shot, the 44-40 recoiling in his arms. In response the pilot banked the helicopter to the east a dozen yards, where the chopper hung poised over the roofs on the opposite side of the street.

What was the polecat waiting for?

Hickok lowered the rifle and fumed. He needed to draw the helicopter in closer to the warehouse.

The aircraft didn't budge.

How could he goad the pilot into coming nearer? Hickok asked himself, then smirked. He extended his left hand, made a fist, and flipped his middle finger up.

Evidently the pilot got the message, because the next instant the helicopter swooped down at the Warrior, its machine guns chattering.

Hickok whirled and scampered toward the entrance. Bullets smacked into the ground all around him, and bits of the road and dirt peppered his buckskins. Midway to the drum wall he stumbled when a searing pain racked his left thigh, and he went down on his knees. He glanced at the descending chopper, then at the drums, at the gap where the SEAL's grill was visible, and wondered why Geronimo hadn't fired. A few more seconds and the craft would be too close to the warehouse to risk trying to destroy it.

Fire! he was tempted to shout.

The machine guns abruptly ceased.

Which could only mean one thing. Hickok dove to the right and rolled, his intuition warning him that the Russian pilot was about to employ a rocket, and after two yards he came to a rest on his back in time to witness an event he hadn't anticipated.

The SEAL launched its rocket.

But so did the chopper.

Geronimo unleashed the van's rocket a millisecond before the pilot fired. Right on target, the rocket flashed into the copter's cockpit and exploded. A heartbeat later the Soviet rocket struck the drum wall.

It all happened so incredibly fast, Hickok could do no more than shout a horrified "No!" He automatically curled into a fetal position, his arms over his head. Caught in the open between the twin blasts, he felt as if a colossal invisible hand smashed him into the depths of an enormous furnace. The heat and the force took his breath away, and for several seconds he thought he would burst into flames. Even with his eyes shut tight, brilliant light engulfed him, penetrating hues of red, orange, and yellow. For the span of 30 seconds he endured the torment of being immersed in a veritable sun. His hair and exposed skin were singed. His lungs were on the verge of rupturing. He thought he was dying.

The sun blinked out.

As suddenly as it began, the ordeal ended. The heat and the wall of force evaporated. Smoke shrouded the area, as thick as the heaviest fog. An acrid scent permeated the air.

Hickok rose to his knees, coughing and rubbing his stinging eyes, ignoring the agony in his left thigh. He placed his left hand on the ground and bumped the Henry, which he scooped up to use as a brace. Propping the stock firmly on the asphalt, he stood. "Geronimo! Marcus! Are you all right?" he yelled.

There was no response.

For one of the few times in his action-packed life, the gunman felt a surge of genuine fear. He hobbled in the direction of the warehouse, swatting at the smoke with his right hand. "Geronimo! Marcus! Where are you?"

They didn't answer.

Hickok's right foot thumped against a jagged piece of metal drum. He angrily kicked it aside and advanced to the verge of the doorway, where the smoke abruptly thinned, permitting him to see the interior. "Dear Spirit!" he breathed, aghast.

The metal drums had taken the brunt of the impact and been

blown to pieces. They had served as a buffer, cushioning the SEAL from the full fury of the explosion, enabling the transport to survive relatively intact. The destructive energy had demolished the ramp and knocked the SEAL a good 15 feet backwards.

Hickok hardly glanced at the van. His attention was riveted on the blood-splattered form lying on the floor eight feet away. The tattered brown clothing, the scorched, lacerated flesh, and the wisps of smoke rising from the blistered scalp brought a lump to his throat. "Marcus!" he croaked, and limped over to the fallen Warrior.

Marcus was flat on his back, his eyes shut, breathing shallowly in ragged breaths. His arms were bent at the elbows and suspended at grotesque angles. Blood flowed from a score of wounds.

"Please. No," Hickok said weakly, and sagged to his knees. "Don't die."

Marcus's eyelids fluttered and his eyes opened. He focused on the gunfighter with a supreme effort. "Hickok?"

"It's me, pard," Hickok assured him, resting his right hand on the gladiator's shoulder. "I'm here."

"I'm glad. I don't want to die alone."

"Don't talk like that," Hickok stated, his voice rasping, sorrow pervading his being.

A door slammed.

The gunman looked up and saw Geronimo walking unsteadily toward them. Blood trickled from a five-inch gash in Geronimo's forehead.

"Hickok?" Marcus said.

"I'm still right here," the gunfighter stated, squeezing Marcus's shoulder gently.

"It's my own fault. I didn't give the signal soon enough. I wanted to be sure."

"You did just fine. We got the damn Commies."

"Good," Marcus said, the word barely audible.

Geronimo joined them, swaying slightly as he halted next to Marcus's head. He took one look and shuddered.

"I feel so tired," Marcus commented.

"Hang in there. I'll get the medicine bag from the buggy," Hickok offered, and started to push himself erect.

"Don't bother," Marcus said softly. A wry grin creased his lips. "You know, I've always wondered what it looks like."

"What?" Hickok asked.

"The other side. The afterlife. Heaven. The mansion worlds. Whatever you want to call it."

Hickok tried to adopt a lighthearted tone. "Don't talk like that," he reiterated. "We'll have you back on your feet in no time."

There were a few seconds of silence.

"You're a rotten liar, Hickok."

The gunman and Geronimo exchanged tormented expressions.

"Give my mom and dad my love," Marcus said. "And tell Blade I'm sorry. I—" he began, then stiffened and arched his back. His gaze seemed to center on something far, far away, and his mouth relaxed in a peaceful smile. He went into eternity with that smile as his parting farewell.

Hickok leaned down and felt for his pulse. He looked up at Geronimo and shook his head.

"I liked him," Geronimo said sadly.

"Are you okay?"

"I cracked my thick skull on the steering wheel, and I keep getting dizzy. I might have a concussion."

"Then you take it easy and I'll handle the burial," Hickok stated, putting his right palm on Marcus's forehead.

"Burial?"

"We're not leavin' him lying here like this."

"You're right," Geronimo said. "We'll take him back with us."

Hickok glanced up. "What are you talkin' about? We're not going back to the Home yet. We've got to rescue Blade."

"We're in no shape to rescue Blade. Look at yourself," Geronimo declared, and pointed at the gunfighter's thigh.

Hickok looked at his leg and grimaced. A pool of blood had formed under him, and the hole in his thigh was large enough to accommodate two of his fingers. "I'll bandage this scratch and we'll head out."

"We're returning to the Home."

"Like hell we are."

Geronimo leaned down and locked his eyes on his best friend. "I don't want to go back either, but we don't have any choice, Nathan. We've lost Marcus. I'm groggy and ready to keel over. And you're bleeding to death. The Healers can take care of us if we return to the Home, but if we try to press on now, in the condition we're in, we'll be committing suicide. We'll never reach Boston." He paused. "You can see I'm right, can't you?"

"But Blade—"

"Blade has been their prisoner for over a week. Another few days won't make a difference if he's still alive. We need to have our injuries tended to and select another Warrior to accompany us," Geronimo said, and sighed. "Do you think I *want* to go back? Do you think I *like* the idea of leaving Blade in their hands? You know me better than that."

Hickok began to object, then changed his mind. He gazed at the blood coating Marcus, the blood seeping down Geronimo's brow, and the blood pumping from his thigh, and his shoulders slumped in agonized resignation. "Damn," he said bitterly.

"We go back?"

"We go back," Hickok stated reluctantly. "Until we heal up, Blade's on his own. I just hope the Big Guy can escape without our help."

Chapter Nineteen

The guard was as easy as pie.

Blade came over the fence at the northwest corner of Gorbachev Air Force Base, scaling the eight-foot-high chainlink barrier effortlessly. The three strands of barbed wire at the top gave him momentary pause, but all he had to do was unsling one of the AK-47's, the one over his left arm, and use the weapon to press down on the strands until they were nearly level with the chain-link portion, then ease his legs over, balancing on his steely arms. A short drop to the ground and he was inside the base, crouched in the inky shadows.

He breathed the cool night air and gazed upward at the stars, thinking of the cab driver he had left loosely bound in the front seat of the taxi, which was parked in a stand of trees situated less than 70 yards to the north of the military post. Harold would eventually free himself and radio for assistance, but the cab driver wouldn't be able to drive off because Blade had flattened all four tires.

Heavy boot steps sounded off to the south.

Blade froze and slowly scanned his immediate vicinity. He

appeared to be at the corner of a runway. Tarmacadam covered the ground. Lampposts were positioned along the fence every 40 feet or so, affording a dim illumination. But, as the Warrior had noted on his wary approach to the fence, the lamps failed to adequately penetrate to the very corner.

A Russian soldier, a perimeter guard, materialized under the nearest lamppost to the south, strolling along the fence and humming contentedly. Over his right shoulder hung an AK-47.

Blade lowered himself to the tarmacadam and waited. If he was lucky the guard wouldn't look down. He'd hoped to reduce the probability of encountering sentries by entering the base after one A.M. So much for his bright idea.

The guard clasped his hands behind his back and stared off in the distance at the lights of a residential neighborhood.

The Warrior released the stock of the AK-47 and eased his right hand to the Bowie on his right hip. He had one important factor working in his favor. The Soviets had controlled Boston for over a century, and not once during that period did they have to contend with an organized rebellion. They had eradicated the last of the lingering bands of freedom fighters in Massachusetts 94 years ago, according to the information Harold had imparted. And since no one had attacked a Russian facility in so long, the Soviet troops were bound to be complacent, bound to be less alert than they would be in a war zone. At least, that's what Blade hoped.

Still humming, the sentry drew ever nearer to the corner. He came within six feet and stopped, turning to gaze over the post. Not far off, to the southwest, were two hangars and a barracks. The first inkling he had that something was wrong, dreadfully wrong, came when a razor point gouged him in the throat and an iron vise clamped on his mouth.

"One word, one twitch, and you're dead."

Petrified, the guard stood stock still, scarcely able to credit his senses.

"I'm going to let go of your mouth. If you try to shout, I'll slit your throat."

The soldier flinched as the knife or bayonet or whatever it

was gouged even deeper into his neck. He exhaled when the hand moved from over his mouth.

"Do you see this?" the man standing directly behind the guard asked.

The sentry's eyes widened in astonishment when the pressure on his throat was relieved and the biggest knife he'd ever seen, maybe the biggest knife in the entire world, was held right in front of his eyes. Even in the dark he could tell the blade must be 14 inches in length. He envisioned the knife sinking into his body and he gulped in fear.

"Do you know what I'll do with this if you don't cooperate?"

"Yes," the guard whispered.

"Where is the HGP Unit?"

The soldier licked his lips and nodded to the southwest. "They're housed in the barracks building next to those two hangers."

"What's in the hangars?"

"The helicopters they use. Eight of them, I think."

"The long-range jobs?"

"There are only two of the modified kind. The others are basic choppers."

"What about the rest of the base personnel and aircraft?"

"All farther south. The HGP Unit has that area all to itself, but most of the base facilities, the barracks where the Air Force personnel are housed, the homes for the married ones and their dependents, the majority of the hangars, and all the rest are located near Airport Road and Hartwell Road, at the south end of the base."

"You've been a great help."

The sentry tensed in anticipation of the knife tearing into him. "Are you going to kill me?" he asked anxiously.

"I want you to relay a message for me," said the man to his rear.

"A message?"

"Yeah. Tell General Malenkov that Blade sends his regards."

"General Malenkov? *The* General Malenkov?"

"You've got it."

Stunned, the guard opened his mouth to voice another question, but a tremendous blow to the back of his head drove him to his knees. The fence and the stars, the whole universe, spun before his eyes. A second blow, delivered on the exact same spot as the first, caused the universe and his consciousness to be devoured by a black hole.

"Thanks for everything," Blade said softly to the figure at his feet. He sheathed the right Bowie and stared at the two hangars and the barracks several hundred yards away, their outlines silhouetted by periodic floodlights. The intelligence the sentry had imparted dovetailed with the layout of the base. Most of the base facilities *were* indeed situated on the south side, as Blade had observed for himself earlier as Harold drove him around the boundary on the roads that came closest to the fence. And it fit that the HGP Unit would be housed in their own barracks, nearer the northern end of the post, away from the regular Air Force troops.

Blade bent down and removed the AK-47 the guard had carried, then picked up the one he'd left on the ground. Now he had three. He slung the assault rifle he'd used to press down the barbed wire, the sme one he'd used during the fight at Krushchev Memorial, the one containing the fewest rounds in its magazine, over his left shoulder.

He was all set.

Blade hunched over and ran toward the buildings, plotting his strategy. Surely at one in the morning most, if not all, of the HGP supersoldiers would be asleep. Doctor Milton had claimed there were 18 of the genetically perfected commandos, and Blade intended to insure they were all dead before he departed Boston. He slowed when he was 50 feet from the three structures, moving silently now, laying his combat boots down softly, studying the setup.

The barracks building was positioned within 20 feet of the west fence and was smaller than the pair of hangars located to its left, both of which were two stories in height and a hundred feet in width. The rear of all three structures faced to the north.

There was no sign of any activity.

Blade padded to within 30 feet of the barracks, his finger on the trigger, the AK-47's on his back sliding slightly with every stride. An important consideration occurred to him. Would the supersoldiers fly their own aircraft or would an Air Force pilot handle the chore? The answer was critical. Elite units normally included whatever specialists were required within their own ranks. The Warriors, as an example he readily thought of, didn't use Tillers to drive the SEAL for them. If the supersoldiers flew their own helicopters, if a few of them had been trained as pilots, then he had his ticket back to the Home.

Muffled conversation abruptly arose from the northwest corner of the barracks.

The Warrior dropped to the tarmacadam and the AK-47 over his right shoulder clattered against the ground.

A pair of soldiers appeared at the corner, a man and a woman, both attired in combat fatigues, both wearing auto pistols in leather holsters strapped to their hips. The woman spoke to the man in Russian and they both took several paces and scanned the runway.

Hidden in the shadows, Blade held his breath. If they spotted him, he'd have to open fire and the shots would alert the supersoldiers inside the barracks. His eyes narrowed. Were those two part of the HGP Unit? Both were well over six feet tall and endowed with strapping physiques. Both had attractive features revealed in the light from a lampost next to the fence. Was he gazing at biologically perfect specimens?

The man addressed the woman, who shrugged. They continued to walk around the rear of the barracks, past a closed door and a blackened window, and passed out of sight when they sauntered between the barracks and the first hangar.

Instantly Blade stood and raced to the northwest corner, his eyes on the window. The lights in the barracks were all out, and for all he knew there could be someone standing in there, watching him. He reached the building without incident and leaned against the wall, pondering. Perhaps the supersoldiers didn't trust the ordinary base guards to protect them properly, or maybe the supersoldiers were required to perform such mundane chores as part of their typical duties. In any event, he had to take them out quickly. He searched the ground and found gravel underfoot. Just what he needed. He grabbed a handful and moved to the northeast corner, doubling over when he went by the window, staying below the sill. At the corner he straightened and peeked past the edge.

The pair were just going around the southeast corner.

Blade slid to the east side of the building, then swiftly laid the three AK-47's alongside the foundation. He inched his right eye to the corner and held his right arm poised to throw the gravel. If the man and woman were making a circuit of the barracks, they'd soon appear at the northwest corner again.

The seconds dragged by, became a minute.

And then they were there, coming slowly around the building, engaged in a quiet discussion.

Blade stepped back, then cast the gravel overhand with all of his strength out over the runway. He drew the Bowies and pressed closer to the building.

The gravel spattered onto the tarmacadam.

An exclamation in Russian came from the male supersoldier. The Warrior heard them talking in hushed tones, and he eased his right eye to the edge once more and peered at the rear of the barracks.

Their hands on their pistols, the pair were advancing across the runway, proceeding carefully, searching for the source of the noise, their backs to the building.

Blade crept after them, doubled in half, the Bowies at his waist, treading lightly. They were engrossed in scrutinizing the runway, exchanging whispered remarks, obviously perplexed but not undully concerned.

Their mistake.

The woman intuitively sensed Blade's presence when he was a stride off, and she spun and started to draw her pistol. He was on her in a flash, his right hand sweeping up and in, the Bowie tearing into her abdomen and carving a grisly path up to her sternum. She grunted and sagged, and Blade had to release the right Bowie in order to confront the man, who had whirled and was just clearing his holster. Knowing he couldn't afford a gunshot, Blade speared the left Bowie into the supersoldier's right wrist and the pistol fell to the ground. Before he could follow through with a body slash, the Russian retreated a pace, then executed a superb spin kick.

Lightning fast, the supersoldier's boot smashed into the left Bowie and knocked the knife from the Warrior's hand.

Surprised by the power in that kick, Blade adopted the horse stance and formed his hands into tiger claws, intending to use a Hung Gar offense to swiftly break through the Russian's guard and dispatch his adversary. But any hopes he entertained of disposing of the supersoldier easily were dashed in the opening moments of their hand-to-hand combat.

Although his right wrist was injured and dripping blood, the HGP commando assumed the Neko-ashi-tachi, the cat stance, and met the Warrior head-on.

Blade let fly with a series of hand and foot strikes, and every one was countered or blocked. He went for the throat repeatedly, and repeatedly his blows were deflected. He tried again and again to shatter a kneecap, and again and again he was thwarted. To his amazement the commando took the initiative, lauching a flurry of superlative karate kicks. Blade blocked a Hidar-mawashi-geri, a left roundhouse kick, then an upper side kick, on the defense now and giving ground to evade the super-soldier's whirling feet.

The commando was a master. He refused to be daunted by the giant's superior size. Any one of his blows would have shattered a brick, and had he been able to land a crippling strike to a nerve center, to a pressure point, to any vulnerable part of the giant's anatomy, the battle would have been promptly ended. But he couldn't and frustration made him uncharacteristically careless. He tried a low kick, aiming at the giant's right shin, and for once his kick landed. The giant started to buckle, his left hand grabbing for his injured leg, exposing the left side to an attack. Which was exactly what the commando wanted. He stepped in close and whipped a Nukite, a piercing hand strike, at the giant's throat.

As Blade hoped he would. The Warrior had deliberately absorbed the punishing kick to his shin to trick the supersoldier into making a fatal mistake. Now he simply snapped his left hand up, batting the Nukite aside, and uncoiled, ramming a palm heel thrust into the commando's jaw.

There was a loud snap and the soldier went rigid as a pole, then collapsed without a sound.

Blade straightened and breathed in deeply. If all the genetically bred commandos were as stalwart and formidable, it was no wonder the Soviets wanted to create as many as they could. A battalion of such supermen and superwomen would be virtually invincible. But all the Soviets had were 16 others, and if Blade had his way they wouldn't have any. He retrieved his left Bowie, walked to the woman and wrenched out his right Bowie, then hurried to the barracks.

The lights were still out inside.

Blade wiped the knives clean on his pants and slid them into their sheaths. A moment later he had two AK-47's slung over his arm and the third gripped in his hands. A cool breeze caressed his skin as he moved to the southeast corner of the barracks and surveyed the structures.

The white front door of the barracks was closed. To his left, parked in front of the nearest hangar, sat a huge tandem helicopter. He remembered Milton saying that the HGP Unit was on alert status 24 hours a day, which meant the Unit had to have a copter ready to go at any hour of the day. Therefore, Blade deduced, the tandem job must be on line and fueled for immediate lift-off.

How convenient.

Blade stalked to the front door and paused. Should he bust it in or try a sneak attack? If he kicked in the door, he'd awaken every commando inside and give them precious seconds to react. The element of surprise was essential to his success.

Oh, well.

Blade tried the knob and found it unlocked. He opened the door slowly to the accompaniment of loud snoring. Since, if an alert sounded, they had to be out the door in minutes, all of the commandos must be asleep within a short distance of the doorway. He slipped into the barracks and eased the door shut, vowing that none of the HGP Unit would get past him alive.

Somewhere someone farted.

The Warrior groped the wall to his right for a light switch. In seconds his probing fingers found it. He stood stock still, girding himself, asserting control over his emotions and his body, willing himself to relax, counting in his mind.

One.

Sixteen to one weren't such bad odds. He'd have the jump on them. The crucial edge.

Two.

If he did die, it wouldn't be without a fight the Russians would long remember. Either way they would require years to rebuild their HGP Unit.

Three.

Blade flicked the switch and overhead lights came on all along the length of the barracks, revealing a desk and several chairs to his left and to his right a room containing sinks, toilets, and showers. Ten feet from the entrance was another door, ajar about eighteen inches, and from behind it came the snoring.

Damn!

The Warrior dashed to the second door, but as he grabbed the knob he heard a gruff voice on the other side.

"Who the hell turned on the lights?"

Blade jerked the door wide and stepped into the sleeping quarters. There were ten bunk beds, five on each side of the room. Only two beds were empty, the two apparently belonging to the pair he'd slain, leaving 18 occupied bunks where there should be only 16 and no time to contemplate the reason for the discrepancy because the commandos were coming alive.

"It's Blade!" the man in the bottom bunk to the Warrior's left shouted, scrambling from under the covers.

"Get him!" chimed in another.

The Warrior sent a half-dozen rounds into the bigmouth to his left and saw the man pitch to the floor, and then he brought the barrel higher to catch the commando in the top bunk, the

heavy slugs flinging the supersoldier from his roost, screeching
in anguish. Blade took two strides into the room, trying to watch
all of the commandos at once, and as he moved he noticed the
black footlockers at the foot of each bunk. Set out neatly on
top of each locker were two camouflage uniforms, except for
the footlocker near the empty bunk and the footlocker next to
the first bed on his right. On that one were *brown* uniforms.
At that moment he also made a chilling observation. Leaning
against the post at the foot of each bunk, with the exception
of the first bunk to his right, were assault rifles, and hanging
from the upright posts were holsters.

All this Blade perceived in the span of three seconds while
the men and women in the bunks struggled to shake the sleep
from their eyes. And then, in a terrible moment of savage action,
the battle was joined.

A woman three bunks down on the left clawed at her AK-47.

Blade shot her in the head, the rounds spraying her brains
and pretty red hair all over the footlocker and the floor. He
strode farther into the room, squeezing the trigger, firing a
steady burst, killing the commando in the bunk above her, then
reversing direction to blast he two men in the second bunk on
the left. Oaths and shouts and screams filled the air. The supersoldiers were all going for their weapons.

A woman in the fourth bunk on the right got hold of her pistol.

His lips a thin, grim line, Blade let her have several rounds
in the chest. He spun to the right and shot the two men in the
second bunk on his right. They thrashed as they were hit,
crimson geysers spurting from their ruined torsos. He swung
around, aiming at the commandos at the back of the barracks,
when the unexpected occurred.

The AK-47 went empty.

In a twinkling he realized there should have been more rounds
in the magazine, and he realized he'd inadvertently used the
same weapon he had employed at the hospital. He tossed the
assault rifle to the right and unslung the AK-47 over his right
shoulder, but even as he did other guns boomed and chattered
and he leaped behind the flimsy cover of the bunk bed to his

left. He'd lost the advantage, and as soon as he showed himself he was dead. The concerted enemy fire would be overwhelming.

Unless.

Unless he met their superior firepower with concentrated firepower of his own.

Bullets were thudding into the bunk above him.

Blade twisted onto his stomach and crawled frantically to the head of the bunks, then turned to the left and squeezed between the next bunk and the wall. The commandos were pouring their shots into the bunk he'd left, unaware of his move, giving him the gift of a moment's breathing space. He quickly unslung the third AK-47, took hold of one in each brawny hand, then rose, firing as he straightened, shooting underneath the top bunk, downing several supersoldiers who were caught by surprise. But he couldn't stand still, not even for an instant, so he darted to the center of the room again, firing as he ran, and he continued to fire once he was in the aisle, sending a burst into a nearby woman, then taking the forehead off a stocky man who lunged at him from the right, and still he fired, swinging the barrels from side to side and up and down, always firing, firing,firing, always in motion, spinning and ducking and weaving. He fired as some of the commandos rushed him. He fired as they sniped at him from behind the bunks. And he fired at the few who attempted to flee out of the rear door. Only the fact that both magazines went empty almost simultaneously stopped him from firing.

An awful silence enveloped the barracks.

Blade threw the assault rifles to the floor and grabbed yet another leaning against a bed to his right. Acrid smoke hung heavy in the room. Bodies were sprawled in the aisle, on the bunks, and near the back door. Blood flowed copiously. Someone groaned.

No one else moved.

But there were two men still alive.

Blade swung toward the first bunk bed on the east side of the room and covered the men who were lying in a state of transfixed terror, the same men who owned the brown uniforms.

Scowling, he stepped over to the bunks. "You don't belong to the HGP Unit. Who are you?"

The dark-haired man in the bottom bunk winced at the raspy, threatening tone in the Warrior's voice, while the man in the top bunk regained his composure, glared defiantly, and crossed his arms.

"I'll never tell you a damn thing!" the defiant one declared.

"Then who needs you?" Blade responded, and shot him.

Startled by the sudden demise of his companion, the dark-haired man held out his arms, as if to ward off a hail of lead, and cried out, "Don't kill me! I'll tell you anything you want to know."

"Do you know who I am?" Blade asked.

"Yeah. The Warrior we picked up in Minnesota."

"Who are you?"

"Captain Jim Nezgorski, Soviet Air Force."

"What are your duties?"

"I'm a pilot. I fly the unit wherever it has to go."

Blade nodded at the corpse in the top bunk. "Was he a pilot too?"

"Yeah."

So elite units usually included specialists within their own ranks? Blade reminded himself of his earlier observation, and shook his head, bemused by his inaccurate insight.

The pilot misconstrued the motion. "I'm not lying. Frank was a pilot. We shared the flight duties."

Blade leaned forward. "I believe you. Now get out of bed."

Jim Nezgorski blinked a few times. "What? Why?"

"That helicopter I saw outside is fueled and ready to take off, isn't it?"

The man hesitated, as if he was about to lie, but he decided, after a glance at the carnage the giant had caused, to tell the truth. "Yeah."

"Then grab your uniform and let's go. Someone was bound to have heard all the noise. Reinforcements will be arriving in less than five minutes. I want us in the air in two."

"Two?" Nezgorski said, and scrambled from bed. He wore

a pair of white boxer shorts. Nervously moving to the front of
the bunks, he snatched a brown uniform from off the footlocker
and went to put it on.

"You can do that after we're airborne," Blade told him, and
wagged the AK-47 at the front door. "Move it."

"My shoes," the pilot declared. He knelt to pull a pair of
brown shoes from under the bed.

Blade covered him, then gestured impatiently when Nezgorski
straightened. "Now get your butt in gear. If we're caught, I
promise you that you'll die before I do. You have one minute
and fifty seconds to lift off."

The pilot hurried toward the entrance. "What then? Where
am I taking you?"

"After we're up, you'll destroy the hangars—"

"I'll what?" Nezgorski blurted out, and stopped.

Blade prodded him with the barrel and the man hustled to
the door. "You'll destroy the hangars and all the aircraft in them
so your Air Force pals won't be able to use the other choppers
to come after us. Is that helicopter outside one of the modified
jobs?"

Nezgorski looked at the Warrior. "How did you know about
them?" he asked, then quickly added, "Yeah. It's one of those
with extended-flight capability."

"So if we blow up the other one, they'll never catch us,"
Blade predicted.

"And after I destroy the hangars?"

"Home, James. Home."

Three Weeks Later

He found the gunman at the small cemetery plot located in the northeast corner of the Home, near the gently flowing inner moat. Birds chirped in the surrounding trees, and a warm breeze blew in from the west.

Hickok stood next to a recently constructed marker, staring at a mound of dirt, his hands clasped at his waist, his features downcast. New patches covered holes in his buckskins, one on his left leg and the other on his left shoulder.

"Nathan?"

The gunfighter turned and smiled wanly. "How's it going, pard?"

"I've never been happier," Blade answered, joining his friend beside the grave. "Jenny has been spoiling me rotten every day, waiting on me hand and foot. Gabe has been a perfect angel. Maybe I should be captured more often."

Hickok grinned. "Have you recovered from that little stroll of yours?"

"Walking from Detroit Lakes to here wasn't so hard," Blade said. "I was fortunate the helicopter got me as far as Illinois, and that jeep got me from Illinois to Detroit Lake before it broke down.''

"Did those scavengers give you any grief when you swiped their jeep?''

"They objected, but I disposed of their objections," Blade said. "Too bad the jeep gave out when it did. I would have reached the Home that much sooner.''

"The important thing is you showed up before Geronimo, Ares, and I took off to find you," Hickok noted.

Blade motioned at the grave. "Geronimo tells me you've been coming here every day.''

"That mangy Injun is a blabbermouth.''

"Care to talk about it?''

"There's nothing to talk about.''

"Do you blame yourself for Marcus's death?" Blade inquired.

The corners of Hickok's eyes crinkled and his mouth curled downward. "I picked him to go. I knew he was a greenhorn.''

"You had the right idea. His death proves it.''

Hickok looked up. "How do you figure?''

"At least half of the Warriors require more experience, and taking them on runs into the Outlands and elsewhere is the best way for them to acquire the combat seasoning they need. If Marcus had had more experience, he might have given the signal sooner and would still be with us," Blade said. "His death wasn't your fault.''

"If you say so," Hickok responded skeptically.

"In fact," Blade went on, "I intend to implement your policy and start taking the less-experienced Warriors with us from time to time.''

"I'm glad you like the idea, but I can't take the credit. Lynx gave me the brainstorm.''

"Lynx? He never makes a suggestion unless he has an ulterior motive.''

"I reckon he wanted me to take him along," Hickok guessed.

"So, Lynx wants to go on a mission, huh?" Blade said, then chuckled. "Okay. We'll take him.''

"We will?"

"Sure. Last."

For the first time in three weeks, Hickok threw back his head and enjoyed a hearty laugh.